GENERATION X

Also by Douglas Coupland

SHAMPOO PLANET

LIFE AFTER GOD

MICROSERFS

POLAROIDS FROM THE DEAD

GIRLFRIEND IN A COMA

MISS WYOMING

HEY NOSTRADAMUS!

ELEANOR RIGBY

JPOD

THE GUM THIEF

GENERATION A

PLAYER ONE

40
YEARS OF
ORIGINAL
WRITING

GENERATION X
Douglas Coupland

ABACUS

First published in the United States by
St Martin's Press 1991
Published in Great Britain by Abacus in 1992 and 1996
Reprinted 1992, 1993 (three times), 1994 (twice), 1995, 1996,
1997 (three times), 1998 (twice), 1999, 2000, 2001, 2002,
2004, 2005, 2007 (twice), 2008, 2009, 2010, 2011

This edition published by Abacus in 2013

A CIP catalogue record of this book is available
from the British Library

ISBN 978-0-349-13892-3

Typeset in Goudy by M Rules
Printed and bound in Great Britain by
Clays Ltd, St Ives plc

Papers used by Abacus are from well-managed forests
and other responsible sources.

 MIX
Paper from
responsible sources
FSC
www.fsc.org FSC® C104740

Abacus
An imprint of
Little, Brown Book Group
100 Victoria Embankment
London Ec4Y 0DY

An Hachette UK Company
www.hachette.co.uk

www.littlebrown.co.uk

CONTENTS

INTRODUCTION TO THE 2013 EDITION   viii

THE SUN IS YOUR ENEMY   3

OUR PARENTS HAD MORE   11

QUIT RECYCLING THE PAST   15

I AM NOT A TARGET MARKET   20

QUIT YOUR JOB   28

DEAD AT 30 BURIED AT 70   34

IT CAN'T LAST   37

SHOPPING IS NOT CREATING   45

RE CON STRUCT   53

ENTER HYPERSPACE   59

DECEMBER 31, 1999   67

NEW ZEALAND GETS NUKED, TOO   75

MONSTERS EXIST   82

DON'T EAT YOURSELF   89

EAT YOUR PARENTS   92

PURCHASED EXPERIENCES DON'T COUNT   99

REMEMBER EARTH CLEARLY	106
CHANGE COLOUR	111
WHY AM I POOR?	120
CELEBRITIES DIE	125
I AM NOT JEALOUS	137
LEAVE YOUR BODY	141
GROW FLOWERS	149
DEFINE NORMAL	153
MTV NOT BULLETS	163
TRANS FORM	169
WELCOME HOME FROM VIETNAM, SON	172
ADVENTURE WITHOUT RISK IS DISNEYLAND	177
PLASTICS NEVER DISINTEGRATE	187
AWAIT LIGHTNING	197
JAN. 01, 2000	203

"Her hair was totally Indian Woolworth perfume clerk. You know – sweet but dumb – she'll marry her way out of the trailer park some day soon. But the dress was early '60s Aeroflot stewardess – you know – that really sad blue the Russians used before they all started wanting to buy Sonys and having Guy Laroche design their Politburo caps. *And such make-up!* Perfect '70s Mary Quant, with these little PVC floral appliqué earrings that looked like antiskid bathtub stickers from a gay Hollywood tub circa 1956. She really caught the sadness – she was the hippest person there. Totally."

TRACEY, 27

"They're my children. Adults or not, I just can't kick them out of the house. It would be cruel. And besides – they're great cooks."

HELEN, 52

GENERATION XVIX

In a few days I turn fifty and my email inbox is starting to ping with requests for quick interviews hanging on the hook: 'Gen X turns Fifty.' There's a part of me that always knew this day might come – and may come again at sixty and seventy. But what I only ever really wanted from the media age-wise, and what I never got, was to be included in one of those essentially cheesy 'Twenty-in-their-Twenties' articles that are stock in trade of lifestyle magazines. I *know*, but it's what I really wanted, and unfortunately when I finally did something that might make me worthy of a 'Twenty-in-their-Twenties' article, it was too late: *Generation X* was published two months after my thirtieth birthday on 1 March 1991; I had to live with the fact that magazines don't run articles on 'Thirty-in-their-Thirties.' By your thirties you should be doing whatever it is you're supposed to be doing with your life and just get on with it – which is what I suppose happened with me as much as to anyone else.

1991 was over twenty years ago, before not just the Internet but also *email*. I remember worrying about my phone bill each month. And I remember the Kuwait War and I remember no more USSR, and I remember the snow on the ground during that particularly mild winter in Montreal where I was living at the time of *Gen X*'s publication. I also remember waiting for the first copy of the book to arrive. Ask any writer: the true moment of birth is when the FedEx envelope is ripped open and a book is fully midwifed into the world.

Here are a few *Generation X* facts: It was originally going to be called *52 Daffodils* after a story contained within the book. I wonder what life would be like now if I'd done that. My Canadian publisher also declined to publish the book, which forever gave American publishers right of first refusal on new books, which began the myth within the Canadian writing world that I was trying to be American not Canadian. But it took years for me to figure out that that was what was actually happening – there was no Internet to crystalize trends on a dime – trends took place across the span of years, not days. Trends had backlashes and then counter-backlashes that also went on for years. These days a meme is good for a few days or a few weeks, max.

So, back to March of 1991, and waiting for the book to arrive. It finally did, but not by FedEx, rather, it arrived via a subcontracted delivery agency that was several weeks late and dropped two books off at the door with a big gash along their right sides. The covers of the books also had folded edge flaps, except the machine that did the edge flapping goofed and the pages of the book stuck out a half inch and looked ridiculous. All in all you couldn't have asked for a more depressing book birth. I phoned my editor in New York and he knew exactly how bad the binding and printing was, and he did that thing people do when they know they've done something wrong, which is to say, he turned it around and got mad at me for being so picky.

So that was March of 1991. The 1980s were over and I had this sadness that some dimension of history, a certain kind of potency, was over . . . that somehow as a culture we'd reached a point where we couldn't count on decades to create looks and feels and tones the way the sixties, seventies or eighties did. I think it's called pattern fatigue, and meanwhile, Francis Fukuyama was declaring the end of history. The art world was dead. Life felt stagnant.

And then Grunge happened.

And then the Internet arrived.

And then the decade began generating, for lack of a better word, decade-osity. The nineties felt like the nineties in a real and good way. Through a stroke of good fate, the same editor who tried to downplay the book's botched first printing *did* have the foresight to choose the name *Generation X* from the list of alternates to *52 Daffodils*. And because of this, the years 1991 to 2000 were far more action-packed than they were in some other parallel universe with a different title.

There was a lot of absurd stuff that went on during that decade. I think most everyone remembers the endless articles on Generation X as an idea . . . what *is* it? Who *are* they? Does Generation X even *exist*? If so, how can we make *money* from it? Are they boomers or are they different? Do they require a different management style?

And on and on.

I've never had an answer to any of these questions, although, as a short-hand, I said, and continue to say, that if you like the Talking Heads back in the day, then you're probably X. Or if you liked New Order. Or Joy Division. Or something, *anything*, other than that wretched Forrest Gumpy baby-boomer we-run-the-planetty crap that boomers endlessly yammer on about – I mean, good for them, have and enjoy your generation! – but please don't tell me that that's me, too, because it's not, it never was and it never will be. The whole point of *Gen X* was, and continues to be, a negation of being forced into Baby Boomerdom against one's will.

And of course there's . . . *sigh* . . . Generation Y, or, rather, Gen Y, which is much more loveable than Generation X because Gen Y's parents are those Forrest Gumpy baby-boomery people, and cheerfully for them, Gen Y acts as their mirror and shadow, thus offering them a bonus extra channel through which they can discuss and view themselves. In a demographic sense, Gen Y really is a generation, while X is only a psychographic.

Do you like the Talking Heads, yes or no?

I remember writing the book. I began in November of 1989. In a fit of authorial romance, I used a tiny advance, $22,500, and took out a lease on a small bungalow in Palm Springs (I know, I just used the word bungalow for real in a sentence) that I regretted the moment I arrived. Palm Springs wasn't anything in 1989. It wasn't mid-century-modern, it wasn't Coachella Festival, it wasn't gay and it wasn't trendy, groovy, hip or anything else. It was a sci-fi like world where an invisible glass dome landed atop a luxury community a week before Richard Nixon's resignation, and I was one of the first explorers to be allowed back into the place after the dome's removal. This was a coincidence. I just thought Palm Springs would be a cheap, pleasant (and yes, romantic) place to write a novel. I didn't realize until I got there how it was an embodiment of a long-outdated way of viewing the world, one where the acme of existence was to ride shotgun in Bob Hope's golf cart, or to sniff the swimming pool chlorine off of Kim Novak's neck. I was the only person under the age of fifty-five who wasn't working in a hospital or a hotel, and even at that, people my age were scarce. There were only two delis where you could get a coffee – as if coffee availability is a measure of anything – but it was this fantasmagorically unhip kingdom I was stuck living in because I was locked into a lease in the state of California, and to break that lease would be credit suicide. So during very lonely days I drove around the highways and dead subdivisions, and golf courses, and secluded desert shotgun practice sites in my Volkswagen Type-3 fastback that had neither an air-conditioner nor a stereo – and I used a battery-powered cassette recorder and played The Stone Roses or Morrissey or usually British bands who felt like they were speaking to me from another galaxy.

While I was writing the book, I thought there would be, at most, a few people who I attended school with in Vancouver, who might *kind of* get what I was writing about – or maybe a few people down in Seattle which was a little bit like Vancouver back then. I was surprised and remain surprised to this day that so many people clicked with X – or with any of the books I've written – because it always seems, in the end, that writing is such a desolate, lonely profession and it never gets less lonely, in fact, as I sit here a few days before turning fifty, it feels so lonely that I wonder if I can visit the place of writing any more – which, in a backward way, tells me that's exactly why I should go forward. The things worth writing about, and the things worth reading about, are the things that feel almost beyond description at the start and are, because of that, frightening.

Fifty? Bring it on, buster!

Douglas Coupland

PART ONE

THE SUN
IS YOUR
ENEMY

Back in the late 1970s, when I was fifteen years old, I spent every penny I then had in the bank to fly across the continent in a 747 jet to Brandon, Manitoba, deep in the Canadian prairies, to witness a total eclipse of the sun. I must have made a strange sight at my young age, being pencil thin and practically albino, quietly checking into a TraveLodge motel to spend the night alone, happily watching snowy network television offerings and drinking glasses of water from glass tumblers that had been washed and rewrapped in paper sheaths so many times they looked like they had been sandpapered. ¶But the night soon ended, and come the morning of the eclipse, I eschewed tour buses and took civic bus transportation to the edge of town. There, I walked far down a dirt side road and into a farmer's field – some sort of cereal that was chest high and corn green and rustled as its blades inflicted small paper burns on my skin as I walked through them. And in that field, when the appointed hour, minute, and second of the darkness came, I lay myself down on the ground, surrounded by the tall pithy grain stalks and the faint sound of insects, and held my breath, there experiencing a mood that I have never really been able to shake completely – a mood of darkness and inevitability and fascination – a mood that surely must have been held by most young people since the dawn of time as they have crooked their necks, stared at the heavens, and watched their sky go out.

One and a half decades later my feelings are just as ambivalent and I sit on the front lanai of my rented bungalow in Palm Springs, California, grooming my two dogs, smelling the cinnamon nighttime pong of snapdragons and efficient whiffs of swimming pool chlorine that drift in from the courtyard while I wait for dawn.

I look east over the San Andreas fault that lies down the middle of the valley like a piece of overcooked meat. Soon enough the sun will explode over that fault and into my day like a line of Vegas showgirls bursting on stage. My dogs are watching, too. They know that an event of import will happen. These dogs, I tell you, they are so smart, but they worry me sometimes. For instance, I'm plucking this pale yellow cottage cheesy guck from their snouts, rather like cheese atop a microwaved pizza, and I have this horrible feeling, for I suspect these dogs (even though their winsome black mongrel eyes would have me believe otherwise) have been rummaging through the dumpsters out behind the cosmetic surgery center again, and their snouts are accessorized with, dare I say, yuppie liposuction fat. *How* they manage to break into the California state regulation coyote-proof red plastic flesh disposal bags is

USE JETS
WHILE YOU
STILL
CAN

beyond me. I guess the doctors are being naughty or lazy. Or both.

This world.

I tell you.

From inside my little bungalow I hear a cupboard door slam. My friend Dag, probably fetching my other friend Claire a starchy snack or a sugary treat. Or even more likely, if I know them, a wee gin and tonic. They have habits.

Dag is from Toronto, Canada (dual citizenship). Claire is from Los Angeles, California. I, for that matter, am from Portland, Oregon, but where you're from feels sort of irrelevant these days ("Since everyone has the same stores in their mini-malls," according to my younger brother, Tyler). We're the three of us, members of the poverty jet set, an enormous global group, and a group I joined, as mentioned earlier, at the age of fifteen when I flew to Manitoba.

Anyhow, as this evening was good for neither Dag nor Claire, they had to come invade my space to absorb cocktails and chill. They needed it. Both had their reasons.

For example, just after 2:00 A.M., Dag got off of shift at Larry's Bar where, along with me, he is a bartender. While the two of us were walking home, he ditched me right in the middle of a conversation we were having and darted across the road, where he then scraped a boulder across the front hood and windshield of a Cutlass Supreme. This is not the first time he has impulsively vandalized like this. The car was the color of butter and bore a bumper sticker saying WE'RE SPENDING OUR CHILDREN'S INHERITANCE, a message that I suppose irked Dag, who was bored and cranky after eight hours of working his McJob ("Low pay, low prestige, low benefits, low future").

I wish I understood this destructive tendency in Dag; otherwise he is such a considerate guy – to the point where once he wouldn't bathe for a week when a spider spun a web in his bathtub.

"I don't know, Andy," he said as he slammed my screen door, doggies in tow, resembling the lapsed half of a Mormon pamphleting duo with a white shirt, askew tie, armpits hinged with sweat, 48-hour stubble, gray slacks ("not pants, *slacks*") and butting his head like a rutting elk almost immediately into the vegetable crisper of my Frigidaire, from which he pulled wilted romaine leaves off the dewy surface of a bottle of cheap vodka, "whether I feel more that I want to punish some aging crock for frittering away my world, or whether I'm just upset that the world has gotten too big – way beyond our capacity to tell stories about it, and so all we're stuck with are these blips and chunks and snippets on bumpers." He chugs from the bottle. "I feel insulted either way."

So it must have been three in the morning. Dag was on a vandal's high, and the two of us were sitting on couches in my living room looking at the fire burning in the fireplace, when shortly Claire stormed in (no knock), her mink-black-bob-cut aflutter, and looking imposing in spite of her shortness, the effect carried off by chic garnered from working the Chanel counter at the local I. Magnin store.

"Date from hell," she announced, causing Dag and I to exchange meaningful glances. She grabbed a glass of mystery drink in the kitchen and then plonked herself down on the small sofa, unconcerned by the impending fashion disaster of multiple dog hairs on her black wool dress.

"Look, Claire. If your date was too hard to talk about, maybe you can use some little puppets and reenact it for us with a little show."

"Fun*nee*, Dag. Fun*nee*. God. *Another* bond peddler and *another* nouvelle dinner of seed bells and Evian water. And, of *course*, he was a survivalist, too. Spent the whole night talking about moving to Montana and the chemicals he's going to put in his gaso*line* tank to keep it all from decomposing. I can't keep doing this. I'll be thirty soon. I feel like a character in a color cartoon."

McJob: A low-pay, low-prestige, low-dignity, low-benefit, no-future job in the service sector. Frequently considered a satisfying career choice by people who have never held one.

She inspected my serviceable (and by no means stunning) furnished room, a space cheered up mainly by inexpensive low-grade Navajo Indian blankets. Then her face loosened. "My date had a low point, too. Out on Highway 111 in Cathedral City there's this store that sells chickens that have been taxidermied. We were driving by and I just about fainted from wanting to have one, they were so cute, but Dan (that was his name) says, 'Now, Claire, you don't *need* a chicken,' to which I said, 'That's not the point, Dan. The point is that I *want* a chicken.' He thereupon commenced giving me this fantastically boring lecture about how the only reason I want a stuffed chicken is because they look so good in a shop window, and that the moment I received one I'd start dreaming up ways to ditch it. True enough. But then I tried to tell him that stuffed chickens are what life and new relationships was all about, but my explanation collapsed somewhere – the analogy became too mangled – and there was that awful woe-to-the-human-race silence you get from pedants who think they're talking to half-wits. I wanted to throttle him."

"Chickens?" asked Dag.

"Yes, chickens."

"Well."

"Yes."

"Cluck cluck."

Things became both silly and morose and after a few hours I retired to the lanai where I am now, plucking possible yuppie fat from the snouts of my dogs and watching sunlight's first pinking of the Coachella Valley, the valley in which Palm Springs lies. Up on a hill in the distance I can see the saddle-shaped form of the home that belongs to Mr. Bob Hope, the

---

Poverty Jet Set: A group of people given to chronic traveling at the expense of long-term job stability or a permanent residence. Tend to have doomed and extremely expensive phone-call relationships with people named Serge or Ilyana. Tend to discuss frequent-flyer programs at parties.

entertainer, melting like a Dali clock into the rocks. I feel calm because my friends are nearby.

"Polyp weather," announces Dag as he comes and sits next to me brushing sage dust off the rickety wood stoop.

"That is just too sick, Dag," says Claire sitting on my other side and putting a blanket over my shoulders (I am only in my underwear).

"Not sick at all. In fact, you should check out the sidewalks near the patio restaurants of Rancho Mirage around noon some day. Folks shedding polyps like dandruff flakes, and when you walk on them it's like walking on a bed of Rice Krispies cereal."

I say, "Shhhh . . ." and the five of us (don't forget the dogs) look eastward. I shiver and pull the blanket tight around myself, for I am colder than I had realized, and I wonder that all things seem to be from hell these days: dates, jobs, parties, weather . . . . Could the situation be that we no longer believe in that particular place? Or maybe we were all promised heaven in our lifetimes, and what we ended up with can't help but suffer in comparison.

Maybe someone got cheated along the way. I wonder.

You know, Dag and Claire smile a lot, as do many people I know. But I have always wondered if there is something either mechanical or malignant to their smiles, for the way they keep their outer lips propped up seems a bit, not false, but *protective*. A minor realization hits me as I sit with the two of them. It is the realization that the smiles that they wear in their daily lives are the same as the smiles worn by people who have been good-naturedly fleeced, but fleeced nonetheless, in public and on a New York sidewalk by card sharks, and who are unable because of social convention to show their anger, who don't want to look like poor sports. The thought is fleeting.

The first chink of sun rises over the lavender mountain of Joshua, but the three of us are just a bit too cool for our own good; we can't just let the moment happen. Dag must greet this flare with a question for us, a gloomy aubade: "What do you think of when you see the sun? Quick. Before you think about it too much and kill your response. Be honest. Be gruesome. Claire, you go first."

Claire understands the drift: "Well, Dag. I see a farmer in Russia, and he's driving a tractor in a wheat field, but the sunlight's gone bad on him – like the fadedness of a black-and-white picture in an old *Life* magazine. And another strange phenomenon has happened, too: rather than sunbeams, the sun has begun to project the odor of old *Life* magazines instead, and the odor is killing his crops. The wheat is thinning as we speak. He's slumped over the wheel of his tractor and he's crying. His wheat is dying of history poisoning."

"Good, Claire. Very weird. And Andy? How about you?"

"Let me think a second."

"Okay, I'll go instead. When I think of the sun, I think of an Australian surf bunny, eighteen years old, maybe, somewhere on Bondi Beach, and discovering her first keratosis lesion on her shin. She's screaming inside her brain and already plotting how she's going to steal Valiums from her mother. Now *you* tell *me*, Andy, what do you think of when you see the sun?"

I refuse to participate in this awfulness. I refuse to put people in my vision. "I think of this place in Antarctica called Lake Vanda, where the rain hasn't fallen in more than two million years."

"Fair enough. That's all?"

"Yes, that's all."

Historical Underdosing: To live in a period of time when nothing seems to happen. Major symptoms include addiction to newspapers, magazines, and TV news broadcasts.

Historical Overdosing: To live in a period of time when too much seems to happen. Major symptoms include addiction to newspapers, magazines, and TV news broadcasts.

There is a pause. And what I *don't* say is this: that this is also the same sun that makes me think of regal tangerines and dimwitted butterflies and lazy carp. And the ecstatic drops of pomegranate blood seeping from skin fissures of fruits rotting on the tree branch next door – drops that hang like rubies from their old brown leather source, alluding to the intense ovarian fertility inside.

The carapace of coolness is too much for Claire, also. She breaks the silence by saying that it's not healthy to live life as a succession of isolated little cool moments. "Either our lives become stories, or there's just no way to get through them."

I agree. Dag agrees. We know that this is why the three of us left our lives behind us and came to the desert – to tell stories and to make our own lives worthwhile tales in the process.

OUR
PARENTS
HAD MORE

"Strip." ¶"Talk to yourself." ¶"Look at the view." ¶"Masturbate." ¶It's a day later (well, actually not even twelve hours later) and the five of us are rattling down Indian Avenue, headed for our afternoon picnic up in the mountains. We're in Dag's syphilitic old Saab, an endearingly tinny ancient red model of the sort driven up the sides of buildings in Disney cartoons and held together by Popsicle sticks, chewing gum and Scotch tape. And in the car we're playing a quick game – answering Claire's open command to "name all of the activities people do when they're by themselves out in the desert." ¶"Take nude Polaroids." ¶"Hoard little pieces of junk and debris." ¶"Shoot those little pieces of junk to bits with a shotgun." ¶"Hey," roars Dag, "it's kind of like life, isn't it?" ¶The car rolls along. ¶"Sometimes," says Claire, as we drive past the I. Magnin where she works, "I develop this weird feeling when I watch these endless waves of gray hair gobbling up the jewels and perfumes at work. I feel like I'm watching this enormous dinner table surrounded by hundreds of greedy little children who are so spoiled, and so impatient, that they can't even wait for food to be prepared. They have to reach for live animals placed on the table and suck the food right out of them."

Okay, okay. This is a cruel, lopsided judgment of what Palm Springs really is – a small town where old people are trying to buy back their youth and a few rungs on the social ladder. As the expression goes, we spend our youth attaining wealth, and our wealth attaining youth. It's really not a bad place here, and it's undeniably lovely – hey, I *do* live here, after all.

But the place makes me worry.

There is no weather in Palm Springs – just like TV. There is also no middle class, and in that sense the place is medieval. Dag says that every time someone on the planet uses a paper clip, fabric softens their laundry, or watches a rerun of "Hee Haw" on TV, a resident somewhere here in the Coachella Valley collects a penny. He's probably right.

Claire notices that the rich people here pay the poor people to cut the thorns from their cactuses. "I've also noticed that they tend to throw out their houseplants rather than maintain them. God. Imagine what their *kids* are like."

Nonetheless, the three of us chose to live here, for the town is undoubtedly a quiet sanctuary from the bulk of middle-class life. And we certainly don't live in one of the dishier neighborhoods the town has to offer. No way. There are neighborhoods here, where, if you see a glint in a patch of crew-cut Bermuda grass, you can assume there's a silver dollar

THE LOVE
OF
MEAT
PREVENTS
ANY REAL
CHANGE

lying there. Where *we* live, in our little bungalows that share a courtyard and a kidney-shaped swimming pool, a twinkle in the grass means a broken Scotch bottle or a colostomy bag that has avoided the trashman's gloved clutch.

The car heads out on a long stretch that heads toward the highway and Claire hugs one of the dogs that has edged its face in between the two front seats. It is a face that now grovels politely but insistently for attention. She lectures into the dog's two obsidian eyes: "*You*, you cute little creature. *You* don't have to worry about having snowmobiles or cocaine or a third house in Orlando, *Florida*. That's right. No *you* don't. You just want a nice little pat on the head."

The dog meanwhile wears the cheerful, helpful look of a bellboy in a foreign country who doesn't understand a word you're saying but who still wants a tip.

"That's right. You wouldn't want to worry yourself with so many *things*. And do you know *why?*" (The dog raises its ears at the inflection, giving the illusion of understanding. Dag insists that all dogs secretly speak the English language and subscribe to the morals and beliefs of the Unitarian church, but Claire objected to this because she said she knew for a *fact*, that when she was in France, the dogs spoke French.) "Because all of those objects would only mutiny and slap you

---

Historical Slumming: The act of visiting locations such as diners, smokestack industrial sites, rural villages – locations where time appears to have been frozen many years back – so as to experience relief when one returns back to "the present."

Brazilification: The widening gulf between the rich and the poor and the accompanying disappearance of the middle classes.

Vaccinated Time Travel: To fantasize about traveling backward in time, but only with proper vaccinations.

in the face. They'd only remind you that all you're doing with your life is collecting objects. And nothing else."

We live small lives on the periphery; we are marginalized and there's a great deal in which we choose not to participate. We wanted silence and we have that silence now. We arrived here speckled in sores and zits, our colons so tied in knots that we never thought we'd have a bowel movement again. Our systems had stopped working, jammed with the odor of copy machines, Wite-Out, the smell of bond paper, and the endless stress of pointless jobs done grudgingly to little applause. We had compulsions that made us confuse shopping with creativity, to take downers and assume that merely renting a video on a Saturday night was enough. But now that we live here in the desert, things are much, *much* better.

QUIT
RECYCLING
THE PAST

At meetings of Alcoholics Anonymous, fellow drinksters will get angry with you if you won't puke for the audience. By that, I mean spill your guts – really dredge up those rotted baskets of fermented kittens and murder implements that lie at the bottoms of all of our personal lakes. AA members want to hear the horror stories of how far you've sunk in life, and no low is low enough. Tales of spouse abuse, embezzlement, and public incontinence are both appreciated and expected. I know this as a fact because I've been to these meetings (lurid details of my own life will follow at a later date), and I've seen the process of onedownmanship in action – and been angry at not having sordid enough tales of debauchery of my own to share. ¶"Never be afraid to cough up a bit of diseased lung for the spectators," said a man who sat next to me at a meeting once, a man with skin like a half-cooked pie crust and who had five grown children who would no longer return his phone calls: "How are people ever going to help themselves if they can't grab onto a fragment of your own horror? People want that little fragment, they *need* it. That little piece of lung makes their own fragments less scary." I'm still looking for a description of storytelling as vital as this.

Thus inspired by my meetings of the Alcoholics Anonymous organization, I instigated a policy of storytelling in my own life, a policy of "bedtime stories," which Dag, Claire, and I share among ourselves. It's simple: we come up with stories and we tell them to each other. The only rule is that we're not allowed to interrupt, just like in AA, and at the end we're not allowed to criticize. This noncritical atmosphere works for us because the three of us are so tight assed about revealing our emotions. A clause like this was the only way we could feel secure with each other.

Claire and Dag took to the game like ducklings to a stream.

"I firmly believe," Dag once said at the beginning, months ago, "that everybody on earth has a deep, dark secret that they'll never tell another soul as long as they live. Their wife, their husband, their lover, or their priest. Never.

"I have my secret. You have yours. Yes, you do – I can see you smiling. You're thinking about your secret right now. Come on: *spill it out*. What is it? Diddle your sister? Circle jerk? Eat your poo to check the taste? Go with a stranger and you'd go with more? Betray a friend? Just tell me. You may be able to help me and not even know it."

Anyhow, today we're going to be telling bedtime stories on our picnic, and on Indian Avenue we're just about to turn off onto the Interstate 10 freeway to head west, riding in the clapped-out ancient red Saab, with Dag at the wheel, informing us that passengers do not really "ride" in his little red car so much as they "motor": "We are motoring off to our picnic in hell."

Hell is the town of West Palm Springs Village – a bleached and defoliated Flintstones color cartoon of a failed housing development from the 1950s. The town lies on a chokingly hot hill a few miles up the valley, and it overlooks the shimmering aluminum necklace of Interstate 10, whose double strands stretch from San Bernardino in the west, out to Blythe and Phoenix in the east.

In an era when nearly all real estate is coveted and developed, West Palm Springs Village is a true rarity: a modern ruin and almost deserted save for a few hearty souls in Airstream trailers and mobile homes, who give us a cautious eye upon our arrival through the town's welcoming sentry – an abandoned Texaco gasoline station surrounded by a chain link fence, and lines of dead and blackened *Washingtonia* palms that seem to have been agent-oranged. The mood is vaguely reminiscent of a Vietnam War movie set.

"You get the impression," says Dag as we drive past the gas station at hearse speed, "that back in, say, 1958, Buddy Hackett, Joey Bishop, and a bunch of Vegas entertainers all banded together to make a bundle on this place, but a key investor split town and the whole place just died."

But again, the village is not entirely dead. A few people do live there, and these few troopers have a splendid view of the windmill ranch down below them that borders the highway – tens of thousands of turbo blades set on poles and aimed at Mount San Gorgonio, one of the windiest places in America. Conceived of as a tax dodge after the oil shock, these windmills are so large and powerful that any one of their blades could cut a man in two. Curiously, they turned out to be functional as well as a good tax dodge, and the volts they silently generate power detox center air conditioners

---

Decade Blending: In clothing: the indiscriminate combination of two or more items from various decades to create a personal mood: *Sheila = Mary Quant earrings (1960s) + cork wedgie platform shoes (1970s) + black leather jacket (1950s and 1980s).*

and cellulite vacuums of the region's burgeoning cosmetic surgery industry.

Claire is dressed today in bubble gum capri pants, sleeveless blouse, scarf, and sunglasses: starlet manqué. She likes retro looks, and she also once told us that if she has kids, "I'm going to give them utterly retro names like Madge or Verna or Ralph. Names like people have in diners."

Dag, on the other hand, is dressed in threadbare chinos, a smooth cotton dress shirt, and sockless in loafers, essentially a reduction of his usual lapsed Mormon motif. He has no sunglasses: he is going to stare at the sun: Huxley redux or Monty Clift, prepping himself for a role and trying to shake the drugs.

"What," ask both my friends, "is this lurid amusement value dead celebrities hold for us?"

Me? I'm just me. I never seem to be able to get into the swing of using "time as a color" in my wardrobe, the way Claire does, or "time cannibalizing" as Dag calls the process. I have enough trouble just being *now*. I dress to be obscure, to be hidden – to be generic. Camouflaged.

So, after cruising around house-free streets, Claire chooses the corner of Cottonwood and Sapphire avenues for our picnic, not because there's anything there (which there isn't, merely a crumbling asphalt road being reclaimed by sage and creosote bushes) but rather because "if you try real hard you can almost feel how optimistic the developers were when they named this place."

The back flap of the car clunks down. Here we will eat chicken breasts, drink iced tea, and greet with exaggerated happiness the pieces of stick and snakeskin the dogs bring to us. And we will tell our bedtime stories to each other under the hot buzzing sun next to vacant lots that in alternately forked universes might still bear the gracious desert homes of such motion picture stars as Mr. William Holden and Miss Grace Kelly. In these homes my two friends Dagmar Bellinghausen and Claire Baxter would be more than welcome for swims, gossip, and frosty rum drinks the color of a Hollywood, California sunset.

But then that's another universe, not this universe. *Here* the three of us merely eat a box lunch on a land that is barren – the equivalent of blank space at the end of a chapter – and a land so empty that all objects placed on its breathing, hot skin become objects of irony. And here, under the big white sun, I get to watch Dag and Claire pretend they inhabit that other, more welcoming universe.

I AM NOT
A TARGET
MARKET

Dag says he's a lesbian trapped inside a man's body. Figure *that* out. To watch him smoke a filter-tipped cigarette out in the desert, the sweat on his face evaporating as quickly as it forms, while Claire teases the dogs with bits of chicken at the back of the Saab's hatch gate, you can't help but be helplessly reminded of the sort of bleached Kodak snapshots taken decades ago and found in shoe boxes in attics everywhere. You know the type: all yellowed and filmy, always with a big faded car in the background and fashions that look surprisingly hip. When you see such photos, you can't help but wonder at just how sweet and sad and innocent all moments of life are rendered by the tripping of a camera's shutter, for at that point the future is still unknown and has yet to hurt us, and also for that brief moment, our poses are accepted as honest. ¶As I watch Dag and Claire piddle about the desert, I also realize that my descriptions of myself and my two friends have been slightly vague until now. A bit more description of them and myself is in order. Time for case studies. ¶I'll begin with Dag. ¶Dag's car pulled up to the curb outside my bungalow about a year ago, its Ontario license plates covered in a mustard crust of Oklahoma mud and Nebraska insects. When he opened the door, a heap of clutter fell out the door and onto the pavement, including a bottle of Chanel Crystalle perfume that smashed. ("Dykes just love Crystalle, you know. So active. So sporty.") I never found out what the perfume was for, but life's been considerably more interesting around here since.

Shortly after Dag arrived, I both found him a place to live – an empty bungalow in between mine and Claire's – and got him a job with me at Larry's Bar, where he quickly took control of the scene. Once, for example, he bet me fifty dollars that he could induce the locals – a depressing froth of failed Zsa Zsa types, low-grade bikers who brew cauldrons of acid up in the mountains, and their biker-bitch chicks with pale-green gang tattoos on their knuckles and faces bearing the appalling complexions of abandoned and rained-on showroom dummies – he bet me he could have them all singing along with him to "It's a Heartache," a grisly, strangely out-of-date Scottish love tune that was never removed from the jukebox, before the night was out. This notion was too silly to even consider, so, of course, I accepted the bet. A few minutes later I was out in the hallway making a long-distance call underneath the native Indian arrowhead display, when suddenly, what did I hear inside the bar but the tuneless bleatings and bellowings of the crowd, accompanied by their swaying beehive do's and waxen edemic biker's arms flailing arrhythmically to the song's beat. Not without admiration, then, did I give Dag his fifty, while a terrifying biker gave him a hug ("I love this guy!"), and then watched Dag put the bill into his mouth, chew it a bit, and then swallow.

"Hey, Andy. You are what you eat."

People are wary of Dag when meeting him for the first time, in the same visceral way prairie folk are wary of the flavor of seawater when tasting it for the first time at an ocean beach. "He has eyebrows," says Claire when describing him on the phone to one of her many sisters.

Dag used to work in advertising (marketing, actually) and came to California from Toronto, Canada, a city that when I once visited gave the efficient, ordered feel of the Yellow Pages sprung to life in three dimensions, peppered with trees and veined with cold water.

"I don't think I was a likable guy. I was actually one of those putzes you see driving a sports car down to the financial district every morning with the roof down and a baseball cap on his head, cocksure and pleased with how frisky and *complete* he looks. I was both thrilled and flattered and achieved no small thrill of power to think that most manufacturers of life-style accessories in the Western world considered me their most desirable target market. But at the slightest provocation I'd have been willing to apologize for my working life – how I work from eight till five in front of a sperm-dissolving VDT performing abstract tasks that indirectly enslave the Third World. But then, hey! Come five o'clock, I'd go nuts! I'd streak my hair and drink beer brewed in Kenya. I'd wear bow ties and listen to *alternative* rock and slum in the arty part of town."

Anyhow, the story of why Dag came to Palm Springs runs through my brain at the moment, so I will continue here with a reconstruction built of Dag's own words, gleaned over the past year of slow nights tending bar. I begin at the point where he once told me how he was at work and suffering from a case of "Sick Building Syndrome," saying, "The windows

BICYCLE COURIER

in the office building where I worked didn't open that morning, and I was sitting in my cubicle, affectionately named the veal-fattening pen. I was getting sicker and more headachy by the minute as the airborne stew of office toxins and viruses recirculated – around and around – in the fans.

"Of course these poison winds were eddying in *my* area in particular, aided by the hum of the white noise machine and the glow of the VDT screens. I wasn't getting much done and was staring at my IBM clone surrounded by a sea of Post-it Notes, rock band posters ripped off of construction site hoarding boards, and a small sepia photo of a wooden whaling ship, crushed in the Antarctic ice, that I once found in an old *National Geographic*. I had placed this photo behind a little gold frame I bought in Chinatown. I would stare at this picture constantly, never quite able to imagine the cold, lonely despair that people who are genuinely trapped must feel – and in the process think better of my own plight in life.

"Anyhow, I wasn't going to produce much, and to be honest, I had decided that morning that it was very hard to see myself doing the same job two years down the road. The thought of it was laughable; *depressing*. So I was being a bit more lax than normal in my behavior. It felt nice. It was pre-quitting elation. I've had it a few times now.

"Karen and Jamie, the 'VDT Vixens' who worked in the veal-fattening pens next to me (we called our area the junior

OFFICE TEMP

stockyard or the junior ghetto, alternately) weren't feeling well or producing much, either. As I remember, Karen was spooked about the Sick Building business more than any of us. She had her sister, who worked as an X-ray technician in Montreal, give her a lead apron, which she wore to protect her ovaries when she was doing her keyboarding work. She was going to quit soon to pick up work as a temp: 'More freedom that way – easier to date the bicycle couriers.'

"Anyway, I remember I was working on a hamburger franchise campaign, the big goal of which, according to my embittered ex-hippie boss, Martin, was to 'get the little monsters so excited about eating a burger that they want to vomit with excitement.' Martin was a forty-year-old *man* saying this. Doubts I'd been having about my work for months were weighing on my mind.

"As luck would have it, that was the morning the public health inspector came around in response to a phone call I'd made earlier that week, questioning the quality of the working environment.

"Martin was horrified that an employee had called the inspectors, and I mean *really* freaked out. In Toronto they can force you to make architectural changes, and alterations are ferociously expensive – fresh air ducts and the like – and health of the office workers be damned, cash signs were dinging up in Martin's eyes, tens of thousands of dollars' worth. He called me into his office and started screaming at me, his teeny-weeny salt and pepper ponytail bobbing up and down, 'I

Veal-fattening Pen: Small, cramped office workstations built of fabric-covered disassemblable wall partitions and inhabited by junior staff members. Named after the small preslaughter cubicles used by the cattle industry.

just don't understand you young people. No workplace is ever okay enough. And you mope and complain about how uncreative your jobs are and how you're getting nowhere, and so when we finally give you a promotion you leave and go pick grapes in Queensland or some other such nonsense.'

"Now Martin, like most embittered ex-hippies, is a yuppie, and I have no idea how you're supposed to relate to those people. And before you start getting shrill and saying yuppies don't exist, let's just face facts: they *do*. Dickoids like Martin who snap like wolverines on speed when they can't have a restaurant's window seat in the nonsmoking section with cloth napkins. Androids who never get jokes and who have something scared and mean at the core of their existence, like an underfed Chihuahua baring its teeny fangs and waiting to have its face kicked in or like a glass of milk sloshed on top of the violet filaments of a bug barbecue: a weird abuse of nature. Yuppies never gamble, they calculate. They have no aura: ever been to a yuppie party? It's like being in an empty room: empty hologram people walking around peeking at themselves in mirrors and surreptitiously misting their tonsils with Binaca spray, just in case they have to kiss another ghost like themselves. There's just nothing *there*.

"So, 'Hey, Martin,' I asked when I go to his office, a plush James Bond number overlooking the downtown core – he's sitting there wearing a computer-generated purple sweater from Korea – a sweater with lots of *tex*ture. Martin likes *tex*ture. 'Put yourself in my shoes. Do you *really* think we enjoy having to work in that toxic waste dump in there?'

Emotional Ketchup Burst: The bottling up of opinions and emotions inside oneself so that they explosively burst forth all at once, shocking and confusing employers and friends – most of whom thought things were fine.

Bleeding Ponytail: An elderly sold-out baby boomer who pines for hippie or pre-sellout days.

"Uncontrollable urges were overtaking me.

"'. . . and then have to watch you chat with your yuppie buddies about your gut liposuction all day while you secrete artificially sweetened royal jelly here in Xanadu?'

"Suddenly I was into this *très* deeply. Well, if I'm going to quit anyway, might as well get a thing or two off my chest.

"'I beg your pardon,' says Martin, the wind taken out of his sails.

"'Or for that matter, do you really think we en*joy* hearing about your brand-new million-dollar *home* when we can barely afford to eat Kraft Dinner sandwiches in our own grimy little shoe boxes and we're pushing *thir*ty? A home you won in a genetic lottery, I might add, sheerly by dint of your having been born at the right time in history? You'd last about ten minutes if you were my age these days, Martin. And I have to endure pinheads like you rusting above me for the rest of my life, always grabbing the best piece of cake first and then putting a barbed-wire fence around the rest. You really make me sick.'

"Unfortunately the phone rang then, so I missed what would have undoubtedly been a feeble retort . . . some higher-up Martin was in the middle of a bum-kissing campaign with and who couldn't be shaken off the line. I dawdled off into the staff cafeteria. There, a salesman from the copy machine

---

Boomer Envy: Envy of material wealth and long-range material security accrued by older members of the baby boom generation by virtue of fortunate births.

Clique Maintenance: The need of one generation to see the generation following it as deficient so as to bolster its own collective ego: *"Kids today do nothing. They're so apathetic. We used to go out and protest. All they do is shop and complain."*

Consensus Terrorism: The process that decides in-office attitudes and behavior.

company was pouring a Styrofoam cup full of scalding hot coffee into the soil around a ficus tree which really hadn't even recovered yet from having been fed cocktails and cigarette butts from the Christmas party. It was pissing rain outside, and the water was drizzling down the windows, but inside the air was as dry as the Sahara from being recirculated. The staff were all bitching about commuting time and making AIDS jokes, labeling the office's fashion victims, sneezing, discussing their horoscopes, planning their time-shares in Santo Domingo, and slagging the rich and famous. I felt cynical, and the room matched my mood. At the coffee machine next to the sink, I grabbed a cup, while Margaret, who worked at the other end of the office, was waiting for her herbal tea to steep and informing me of the ramifications of my letting off of steam a few minutes earlier.

"'What *did* you just say to Martin, Dag?' she says to me. 'He's just having *kittens* in his office – cursing your name up and down. Did the health inspector declare this place a Bho*pal* or something?'"

QUIT
YOUR
JOB

"I deflected her question. I like Margaret. She tries hard. She's older, and attractive in a hair-spray-and-shoulder-pads-twice-divorced survivor kind of way. A real bulldozer. She's like one of those little rooms you find only in Chicago or New York in superexpensive downtown apartments – small rooms painted intense, flaring colors like emerald or raw beef to hide the fact that they're so small. She told me my season once, too: I'm a summer. ¶ "God, Margaret. You really have to wonder why we even bother to get *up* in the morning. I mean, really: *Why work*? Simply to buy more *stuff*? That's just not enough. Look at us all. What's the common assumption that got us all from there to here? What makes us de*serve* the ice cream and running shoes and wool Italian suits we have? I mean, I see all of us trying so hard to acquire so much *stuff*, but I can't help but feel that we didn't merit it, that . . .' ¶ "But Margaret cooled me right there. Putting down her mug, she said that before I got into one of my Exercised Young Man states, I should realize that the only reason we all go to work in the morning is because we're terrified of what would happen if we *stopped*. 'We're not built for free time as a species. We think we are, but we aren't.' Then she began almost talking to herself. I'd gotten her going. She was saying that most of us have only two or three genuinely interesting moments in our lives, the rest is filler, and that at the end of our lives, most of us will be lucky if any of those moments connect together to form a story that anyone would find remotely interesting.

"Well. You can see that morbid and self-destructive impulses were overtaking me that morning and that Margaret was more than willing to sweep her floor into my fireplace. So we sat there watching tea steep (never a fun thing to do, I might add) and in a shared moment listened to the office proles discuss whether a certain game show host had or had not had cosmetic surgery recently.

"'Hey, Margaret,' I said, 'I bet you can't think of one person in the entire history of the world who became famous without a whole lot of cash changing hands along the way.'

"She wanted to know what this meant, so I elaborated. I told her that people simply don't . . . *can't* become famous in this world unless a lot of people make a lot of money. The cynicism of this took her aback, but she answered my challenge at face value. 'That's a bit harsh, Dag. What about Abraham Lincoln?'

"'No go. That was all about slavery and land. Tons-o'-cash happening there.'

"So she says, 'Leonardo da Vinci,' to which I could only state that he was a businessman like Shakespeare or any of those old boys and that all of his work was purely on a commission basis and even *worse*, his research was used to support the military.

"'Well, Dag, this is just the *stu*pidest argument I've ever

Sick Building Migration: The tendency of younger workers to leave or avoid jobs in unhealthy office environments or workplaces affected by the Sick Building Syndrome.

Recurving: Leaving one job to take another that pays less but places one back on the learning curve.

heard,' she starts saying, getting desperate. 'Of course people become famous without people making money out of it.'

"'So name one, then.'

"I could see Margaret's thinking flail, her features dissolving and reforming, and I was feeling just a little too full of myself, knowing that other people in the cafeteria had started to listen in on the conversation. I was the boy in the baseball cap driving the convertible again, high on his own cleverness and ascribing darkness and greed to all human endeavors. That was me.

"'Oh, all right, you win,' she says, conceding me a pyrrhic victory, and I was about to walk out of the room with my coffee (now the Perfect-But-Somewhat-Smug Young Man) when I heard a little voice at the back of the coffee room say 'Anne Frank.'

"Well.

"I pivoted around on the ball of my foot, and who did I see, looking quietly defiant but dreadfully dull and tubby, but Charlene sitting next to the megatub of office acetaminophen tablets. Charlene with her trailer-park bleached perm, meat-extension recipes culled from *Family Circle* magazine, and neglect from her boyfriend; the sort of person who when you draw their name out of the hat for the office Christmas party gift, you say, 'Who?'

"'Anne Frank?' I bellowed, 'Why of *course* there was money there, why . . .' but, of course, there was no money there. I had unwittingly declared a moral battle that she had deftly won. I felt awfully silly and awfully mean.

"The staff, of course, sided with Charlene – no one sides with scuzzballs. They were wearing their 'you-got-your-come-uppance' smiles, and there was a lull while the cafeteria audience waited for me to dig my hole deeper, with Charlene

---

Ozmosis: The inability of one's job to live up to one's self-image.

Power Mist: The tendency of hierarchies in office environments to be diffuse and preclude crisp articulation.

in particular looking righteous. But I just stood there unspeaking; all they got to watch instead was my fluffy white karma instantly converting into iron-black cannon balls accelerating to the bottom of a cold and deep Swiss lake. I felt like turning into a plant – a comatose, nonbreathing, nonthinking entity, right there and then. But, of course, plants in offices get scalding hot coffee poured into their soil by copier machine repair people, don't they? So what was I to do? I wrote off the psychic wreckage of that job, before it got any worse. I walked out of that kitchen, out the office doors, and never bothered to come back. Nor did I ever bother to gather my belongings from my veal-fattening pen.

"I figure in retrospect, though, that if they had *any* wisdom at all at the company (which I doubt), they would have made Charlene clean out my desk for me. Only because in my mind's eye I like to see her standing there, wastepaper basket in her plump sausage-fingered hands, sifting through my rubble of documents. There she would come across my framed photo of the whaling ship crushed and stuck, possibly forever, in the glassy Antarctic ice. I see her staring at this photo in mild confusion, wondering in that moment what sort of young man I am and possibly finding me not unlovable.

"But inevitably she would wonder *why* I would want to frame such a strange image and then, I imagine, she would wonder whether it has any financial value. I then see her counting her lucky stars that she doesn't understand such unorthodox impulses, and then I see her throwing the picture, already forgotten, into the trash. But in that brief moment of confusion . . . *that brief moment* before she'd decided to throw the photo out, well . . . I think I could almost love Charlene then.

"And it was this thought of loving that sustained me for a long while when, after quitting, I turned into a Basement Person and never went in to work in an office again."

"Now: when you become a Basement Person, you drop out of the system. You have to give up, as I did, your above-ground apartment and all of the silly black matte objects inside *as well as* the meaningless rectangles of minimalist art above the oatmeal-colored sofa and the semidisposable furniture from Sweden. Basement People rent basement suites; the air above is too middle class.

"I stopped cutting my hair. I began drinking too many little baby coffees as strong as heroin in small cafés where sixteen-year-old boys and girls with nose rings daily invented new salad dressings by selecting spices with the most exotic names ('*Oooh! Cardamom! Let's try a teaspoon of that!*'). I developed new friends who yapped endlessly about South American novelists never getting enough attention. I ate lentils. I wore llama motif serapes, smoked brave little cigarettes (*Nazionali's*, from Italy, I remember). In short, I was earnest.

"Basement subculture was strictly codified: wardrobes consisted primarily of tie-dyed and faded T-shirts bearing images of Schopenhauer or Ethel and Julius Rosenberg, all accessorized with Rasta doohickeys and badges. The girls all seemed to be ferocious dykey redheads, and the boys were untanned and sullen. No one ever seemed to have sex, saving their intensity instead for discussions of social work and generating the best idea for the most obscure and politically correct travel

---

Overboarding: Overcompensating for fears about the future by plunging headlong into a job or life-style seemingly unrelated to one's previous life interests; i.e., Amway sales, aerobics, the Republican party, a career in law, cults, McJobs. . . .

Earth Tones: A youthful subgroup interested in vegetarianism, tie-dyed outfits, mild recreational drugs, and good stereo equipment. Earnest, frequently lacking in humor.

Ethnomagnetism: The tendency of young people to live in emotionally demonstrative, more unrestrained ethnic neighborhoods: *"You wouldn't understand it there, Mother — they hug where I live now."*

destination (the Nama Valley in Namibia – but *only* to see the daisies). Movies were black and white and frequently Brazilian.

"And after a while of living the Basement life-style, I began to adopt more of its attitudes. I began occupational slumming: taking jobs so beneath my abilities that people would have to look at me and say, 'Well of course he could do *better*.' I also got into cult employment, the best form of which was tree planting in the interior of British Columbia one summer in a not unpleasant blitz of pot and crab lice and drag races in beat-up spray-painted old Chevelles and Biscaynes.

"All of this was to try and shake the taint that marketing had given me, that had indulged my need for control too bloodlessly, that had, in some way, taught me to not really *like* myself. Marketing is essentially about feeding the poop back to diners fast enough to make them think they're still getting real food. It's not creation, really, but theft, and *no one* ever feels good about stealing.

"But basically, my life-style escape wasn't working. I was only using the *real* Basement People to my own ends – no different than the way design people exploit artists for new design riffs. I was an imposter, and in the end my situation got so bad that I finally had my Mid-twenties Breakdown. That's when things got pharmaceutical, when they hit *bottom*, and when all voices of comfort began to fail."

Mid-twenties Breakdown: A period of mental collapse occurring in one's twenties, often caused by an inability to function outside of school or structured environments coupled with a realization of one's essential aloneness in the world. Often marks induction into the ritual of pharmaceutical usage.

DEAD AT 30
BURIED AT
70

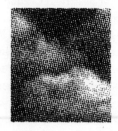

Ever notice how hard it is to talk after you've eaten lunch outside on a super-hot day? A real scorcher? Shimmying palm trees melt in the distance; I absentmindedly stare at the ridges in my fingernails and wonder if I'm receiving sufficient dietary calcium. Dag's story continues. It runs in my head while the three of us eat lunch. ¶"By then it was winter. I moved in with my brother, Matthew, the jingle writer. That was in Buffalo, New York, an hour south of Toronto, and a city which I once read had been labeled North America's first 'ghost city' since a sizable chunk of its core businesses had just up and left one fine 1970s day. ¶"I remember watching Lake Erie freeze over a period of days from Matthew's apartment window and thinking how corny but apt the sight was. Matthew was out of town frequently on business, and I'd sit by myself in the middle of his living room floor with stacks of pornography and bottles of Blue Sapphire gin and the stereo going full blast and I'd be thinking to myself, 'Hey! I'm having a party!' I was on a depressive's diet then – a total salad bar of downers and anti-depressants. I needed them to fight my black thoughts. I was convinced that all of the people I'd ever gone to school with were headed for great things in life and that I wasn't. They were having more fun; finding more meaning in life. I couldn't answer the telephone; I seemed unable to achieve the animal happiness of people on TV, so I had to stop watching it; mirrors freaked me out; I read every Agatha Christie book; I once thought I'd lost my shadow. I was on automatic pilot.

"I became nonsexual and my body felt inside-out – covered with ice and carbon and plywood like the abandoned mini-malls, flour mills, and oil refineries of Tonawanda and Niagara Falls. Sexual signals became omnipresent and remained repulsive. Accidental eye contact with 7-Eleven grocery clerks became charged with vile meaning. All looks with strangers became the unspoken question, 'Are *you* the stranger who will rescue me?' Starved for affection, terrified of abandonment, I began to wonder if sex was really just an excuse to look deeply into another human being's eyes.

"I started to find humanity repulsive, reducing it to hormones, flanks, mounds, secretions, and compelling methanous stinks. At least in this state I felt that there was no possibility of being the ideal target market any more. If, back in Toronto, I had tried to have life both ways by considering myself unfettered and creative, while also playing the patsy corporate drone, I was certainly paying a price.

"But what really got me was the way *young* people can look into your eyes, curious but without a trace of bodily hunger. Early teens and younger, who I'd see looking envy-makingly happy during my brief agoraphobia-filled forays into the local Buffalo malls that were still open. That guileless look had been erased forever in me, so I felt, and I was convinced that I would walk around the next forty years hollowly acting out life's motions, while listening to the rustling, taunting maracas of youthful mummy dust bounce about inside me.

Successophobia: The fear that if one is successful, then one's personal needs will be forgotten and one will no longer have one's childish needs catered to.

"Okay, okay. We all go through a certain crisis point, or, I suppose, we're not complete. I can't *tell* you how many people I know who claim to have had their midlife crisis early in life. But there invariably comes a certain point where our youth fails us; where college fails us; where Mom and Dad fail us. Me, I'd never be able to find refuge again in Saturday mornings spent in rumpus rooms, itchy with fiberglass insulation, listening to Mel Blanc's voice on the TV, unwittingly breathing xenon vapors from cinder blocks, snacking on chewable vitamin C tablets, and tormenting my sister's Barbies.

"But my crisis wasn't just the failure of youth but also a failure of class and of sex and the future and I *still* don't know what. I began to see this world as one where citizens stare, say, at the armless Venus de Milo and fantasize about amputee sex or self-righteously apply a fig leaf to the statue of David, but not before breaking off his dick as a souvenir. All events became omens; I lost the ability to take anything literally.

"So the point of all of this was that I needed a clean slate with no one to read it. I needed to drop out even further. My life had become a series of scary incidents that simply weren't stringing together to make for an interesting book, and God, you get old so quickly! Time was (and is) running out. So I split to where the weather is hot and dry and where the cigarettes are cheap. Like you and Claire. And now I'm here."

IT
CAN'T
LAST

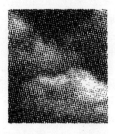

So now you know a bit more about Dag (skewed as his narrative presentation of his life may be). But meanwhile, back at our picnic on this throbbing desert day, Claire is just finishing her mesquite chicken, wiping off her sunglasses, and replacing them with authority on the bridge of her nose indicating that she's getting ready to tell us a story. ¶A bit about Claire here: she has scrawl handwriting like a taxi driver. She knows how to fold Japanese paper cranes and she actually likes the taste of soya burgers. She arrived in Palm Springs on the hot, windy Mother's Day weekend that Nostradamus (according to some interpretations) had predicted would be the end of the world. ¶I was tending the poolside bar at La Spa de Luxembourg then, a far more lofty place than lowly Larry's and a resort complete with nine bubbling health pools and patterned imitation silver knives and forks for outdoor use. Weighty stuff, and it always impressed the guests. Anyhow, I remember watching Claire's incalculably numerous and noisy siblings, half-siblings, step-siblings chatter incessantly out in the sun by the pools, like parakeets in an aviary while a sullen, hungry tomcat prowls outside the cage's mesh. For lunch they would only eat fish, and only tiny fish at that. As one of them said, "The big fish have been in the water a bit too long, and God only *knows* what they've had a chance to eat." And talk about pretense! They kept the same unread copy of the *Frankfurter Allgemeine Zeitung* lying on the table for three days running. I tell you.

At a nearby table, Mr. Baxter, Claire's father, sat with his glistening and be-gemmed business cronies ignoring his progeny, while Mrs. Scott-Baxter, his fourth (and trophy) wife, blonde and young and bored, glowered at the Baxter spawn like a mother mink in a mink farm, just waiting for a jet to strafe the facility, affording her an excuse to feign terror and eat her young.

The whole Baxter clan had *en masse* been imported from L.A. that weekend by the highly superstitious Mr. Baxter, a New Age convert (thanks to wife number three), to avoid a most certain doom in the city. Shakey Angelinos like him were luridly envisioning the strangely large houses of the valley and canyons being inhaled into chinks in the earth with rich glottal slurps and no mercy, all the while being pelleted by rains of toads. A true Californian, he joked: "Hey, at least it's visual."

Claire, however, sat looking profoundly unamused by her family's spirited, italicized conversations. She was idly tethering her paper plate loaded with a low-calorie/high fiber lunch of pineapple bean sprouts and skinless chicken to the outdoor

tabletop while forceful winds, unseasonably fierce, swept down from Mount San Jacinto. I remember the morbid snippets of chitchat that were being prattled around the table by the hordes of sleek and glamorous young Baxters:

"It was *His*ter, not *Hit*ler, Nostradamus predicted," one brother, Allan, a private school Biff-and-Muffy type, yelled across a table, "and he predicted the JFK assassination, *too*."

"I don't remember the JFK assassination."

"I'm wearing a pillbox hat to the end-of-the-world party at Zola's, tonight. Like Jackie. Very historical."

"The hat was a *Hal*ston, you know."

"That's *so* Warhol."

"Dead celebrities are de *fac*to amusing."

"Remember that Halloween a few years ago during the Tylenol tampering scare, when everyone showed up at parties dressed as boxes of Tylenol . . ."

". . . and then looked hurt when they realized they weren't the only ones who'd come up with the idea."

"You know, this is *so* stupid being here because there are three earthquake faults that run right through the city. We might as well paint targets on our shirts."

"Did Nos*trad*amus ever say anything about random snipers?"

"Can you milk horses?"

"What's *that* got to do with anything?"

Their talk was endless, compulsive, and indulgent, sometimes sounding like the remains of the English language after having been hashed over by nuclear war survivors for a few hundred years. But then their words so strongly captured the spirit of the times, and they remain in my mind:

Safety Net-ism: The belief that there will always be a financial and emotional safety net to buffer life's hurts. Usually parents.

Divorce Assumption: A form of *Safety Net-ism*, the belief that if a marriage doesn't work out, then there is no problem because partners can simply seek a divorce.

"I saw a record producer in the parking lot. He and wifey were heading to *Utah*. They said this place was a disaster area, and only Utah was safe. They had this really hot gold Corniche, and in the trunk they had cartons of freeze-dried army food and bottled water from Alberta. Wifey looked really scared."

"Did you see the pound of plastic lipofat in the nurse's office? Just like the fake food in sushi restaurant windows. Looks like a dish of raspberry kiwi fruit puree."

"Someone turn off the wind machine, for Chrissake, it's like a fashion shoot out here."

"Stop being such a male model."

"I'll hum some Eurodisco."

(Paper plates loaded with beef and chutney and baby vegetables were, at that point, gliding off the bright white tables, and into the pool.)

"Ignore the wind, Davie. Don't cosign nature's bullshit. It'll go away."

"Hey . . . is it possible to damage the sun? I mean, we can wreck just about anything we want to here on earth. But can we screw up the sun if we wanted to? I don't know. *Can* we?"

"I'm more worried about computer viruses."

Claire got up and came over to the bar where I was working to pick up her trayload of Cape Cods ("More Cape than Cod, please") and made a shrugging, "*My family, zheeesh!*" gesture. She then walked back to the table, showing me her back, which was framed by a black one-piece swimsuit – a pale white back bearing a Silly Putty-colored espalier of scars.

Anti-sabbatical: A job taken with the sole intention of staying only for a limited period of time (often one year). The intention is usually to raise enough funds to partake in another, more personally meaningful activity such as watercolor sketching in Crete or designing computer knit sweaters in Hong Kong. Employers are rarely informed of intentions.

These were remnants, I discovered later on, of a long-past childhood illness that immobilized her for years in hospitals spanning from Brentwood to Lausanne. In these hospitals doctors tapped vile viral syrups from her spine and in them she also spent the formative years of her life conversing with healing invalid souls – institutional borderline cases, the fringed, and the bent ("To this day, I prefer talking with incomplete people; they're more complete").

But then Claire stopped in midmotion and came back to the bar, where she lifted her sunglasses and confided to me, "You know, I really think that when God puts together families, he sticks his finger into the white pages and selects a group of people at random and then says to them all, 'Hey! You're going to spend the next seventy years together, even though you have nothing in common and don't even *like* each other. *And*, should you not feel yourself caring about any of this group of strangers, *even for a second*, you will feel just *dreadful.*' That's what I think. What about you?"

History does not record my response.

She delivered the drinks to her family, who delivered a chorus of "*Thanks, Spinster*," and then returned. Her hair then, as now, was cut short and Boopishly bobbed, and she wanted to know what on earth I was doing in Palm Springs. She said that anyone under the age of thirty living in a resort community was on the make somehow: "pimping, dealing, hooking, detoxing, escaping, scamming, or what have you." I obliquely told her I was merely trying to erase all traces of history from my past, and she took that at face value. She then described her own job in L.A. while sipping her drink, absentmindedly scanning her complexion for *arriviste* pimples in her reflection in the mirrored shelf behind me.

"I'm a garment buyer – daywear" she fessed up, but then admitted that fashion was only a short-term career. "I don't think it's making me a better person, and the garment business is *so* jammed with dishonesty. I'd like to go somewhere rocky, somewhere Mal*tese*, and just empty my brain, read books, and be with people who wanted to do the same thing."

This was the point where I planted the seed that soon bore such unexpected and wonderful fruit in my life. I said, "Why don't you move *here*. Quit everything." There was a friendliness between us that made me worrilessly continue: "Clean your slate. Think life out. Lose your unwanted momentums. Just think of how therapeutic it could be, and there's an empty bungalow right next to my place. You could move in tomorrow and I know *lots* of jokes."

"Maybe I will," she said, "maybe I will." She smiled and then swung to look at her family, as ever preening and chatting away, arguing about the reported length of John Dillinger's member, discussing the demonic aspects of Claire's stepsister Joanne's phone number – which contained three sixes in a row – and more about the dead Frenchman Nostradamus and his predictions.

"Look at them, will you? Imagine having to go to Disneyland with all of your brothers and sisters at the age of twenty-*seven*. I can't be*lieve* I let myself get dragged into this. If the wind doesn't knock this place down first, it'll implode from a lack of hipness. You have brothers and sisters?"

I explained that I have three of each.

"So you *know* what it's like when everyone starts carving up the future into nasty little bits. God, when they start talking like that – you know all of this sex gossip and end-of-the-world nonsense, I wonder if they're really only confessing something else to each other."

"Like?"

"Like how scared sick they all are. I mean, when people start talking seriously about hoarding cases of Beef-a-Roni in the garage and get all misty-eyed about the Last Days, then it's about as striking a confession as you're ever likely to get of how upset they are that life isn't working out the way they thought it would."

I was in heaven! How could *I not* be, after finding someone who likes to talk like this? So we continued on in this vein for an hour, maybe, interrupted only by my serving the occasional rum drink and Allan's arrival to grab a dish of smoked almonds and to slap Claire on the back: "Hey, Mister – is Spinster putting the make on you?"

"Allan and my family consider me a freak because I'm not married yet," she told me and then turned to pour her pink Cape Cod cocktail down his shirt. "And stop using that awful name."

Allan didn't have time to retaliate, though. From Mr. Baxter's table there arose a commotion as one of the seated bodies slumped and a flurry of middle-age men with tans, paunches, and much jewelry crossed themselves and gathered around that slumped body – Mr. Baxter with a hand clutched to his chest and eyes wide, resembling those of Cocoa, the velvet painting clown.

"Not *again*," said Allan and Claire in unison.

"You go this time? Allan. It's *your* turn."

Allan, dripping juice, grudgingly headed over toward the commotion, where several people were claiming to have already alerted the paramedics.

"Excuse me, Claire," I said, "but your father looks like he's had a heart attack or something. Aren't you being slightly, oh, I don't know . . . *bloodless* about the matter?"

"Oh, Andy. Don't worry. He does this three times a year – just as long as he has a big audience."

It was a busy little scene, that poolside, but you could tell the Baxters amid the chaos by their lack of concern with the excitement, pointing languidly toward the hubbub when the two paramedics and their trolley (a familiar sight in Palm Springs) arrived. There, they loaded Mr. Baxter onto the trolley, after having told a novice Mrs. Scott-Baxter to stop trying to stuff quartz crystals into his hand (she was a New Ager, too), carted him away, only to hear loud clanging sounds that stopped the whole poolside crowd in their tracks. Looking over toward the cart they saw that several items of tableware had fallen out of Mr. Baxter's pocket. His ashen face looked mortified and the silence was both incandescent and painful.

"Oh, *Dad*," said Allan, "How could you em*bar*rass us like

this?" he then said, picking up a piece and looking at it appraisingly. "It's obviously only *plate*. Haven't we trained you properly?"

The taut cord of tension broke. There were laughs, and Mr. Baxter was carted away, only to be treated for what turned out in the end to be a genuinely perilous heart attack after all. Claire meanwhile, I noticed peripherally, sitting over on the edge of one of the ocher-silted mineral pools, her feet dangling in the honey-colored murk of water and staring at the sun, now almost set over the mountain. In her small voice she was talking to the sun and telling it she was very sorry if we'd hurt it or caused it any pain. I knew then that we were friends for life.

SHOPPING
IS NOT
CREATING

The dogs are already pooped from the heat and lying in the shadow of the Saab, chasing dream bunnies with twitching back legs. Dag and I, both being in a carbohydrate coma, aren't far behind and are in a good listening mood as Claire begins her story of the day. ¶"It's a Texlahoma story," she says, much to our pleasure, for Texlahoma is a mythic world we created in which to set many of our stories. It's a sad Everyplace, where citizens are always getting fired from their jobs at the 7-Eleven and where the kids do drugs and practice the latest dance crazes at the local lake, where they also fantasize about being adult and pulling welfare-check scams as the inspect each other's skin for chemical burns from the lake water. Texlahomans shoplift cheap imitation perfumes from dime stores and shoot each other over Thanksgiving dinners every year. And about the only good thing that happens there is the cultivation of cold, unglamorous wheat in which Texlahomans take a justifiable pride; by law, all citizens must put bumper stickers on their cars saying: NO FARMERS: NO FOOD. ¶Life is boring there, but there are some thrills to be had: all the adults keep large quantities of cheaply sewn scarlet sex garments in their chests of drawers. These are panties and ticklers rocketed in from Korea – and I say rocketed in because Texlahoma is an asteroid orbiting the earth, where the year is permanently 1974, the year after the oil shock and the year starting from which real wages in the U.S. never grew ever again. The atmosphere contains oxygen, wheat chaff, and A.M. radio transmissions. It's a fun place to spend one day, and then you just want to get the hell out of there.

Anyhow, now that you know the setting, let's jump into Claire's story.

"This is a story about an astronaut named Buck. One afternoon, Buck the Astronaut had a problem with his spaceship and was forced to land in Texlahoma – in the suburban backyard of the Monroe family. The problem with Buck's spacecraft was that it wasn't programmed to deal with Texlahoma's gravity – the people back on Earth had forgotten to tell him that Texlahoma even existed!

"'That always happens,' said Mrs. Monroe, as she led Buck away from the ship and past the swing set in the backyard toward the house, 'Cape Canaveral just plum forgets that we're here.'

"Being the middle of the day, Mrs. Monroe offered Buck a hot nutritious lunch of cream of mushroom soup meatballs and canned niblet corn. She was glad to have company: her three daughters were at work, and her husband was out on the thresher.

"Then, after lunch, she invited Buck into the parlor to watch TV game shows with her. 'Normally I'd be out in the garage working on my inventory of aloe products that I represent, but business is kind of slow right now.'

"Buck nodded his concurrence.

"'You ever thought of being a rep for aloe products after you retire from being an astronaut, Buck?'

"'No, ma'am,' said Buck, 'I hadn't.'

"'Give it a thought. All you have to do is get a chain of reps working under you, and before you know it, you don't have to work at all – just sit back and skim the profit.'

"'Well, I'll be darned,' said Buck, who also complimented Mrs. Monroe on her collection of souvenir matchbooks placed in an oversized brandy snifter on the parlor table.

"But suddenly something went wrong. Right before Mrs. Monroe's eyes, Buck began to turn pale green, and his head began to turn boxy and veined, like Frankenstein's. Buck raced to look at a little budgie mirror, the only mirror available, and knew instantly what had happened: he had developed space poisoning. He would start to look like a monster, and shortly, he would fall into an almost permanent sleep.

"Mrs. Monroe immediately assumed, however, that her cream of mushroom soup meatballs had been tainted and that as a result of her culinary shortcomings, she had ruined Buck's adorable astronaut's good looks, and possibly his career. She offered to take him to the local clinic, but Buck deferred.

"'That's probably for the best,' said Mrs. Monroe, 'considering that all there is at the clinic is peritonitis vaccinations and a jaws of life.'

"'Just show me a place where I can fall down to sleep,' Buck said, 'I've come down with space poisoning, and within

---

Legislated Nostalgia: To force a body of people to have memories they do not actually possess: *"How can I be a part of the 1960s generation when I don't even remember any of it?"*

Now Denial: To tell oneself that the only time worth living in is the past and that the only time that may ever be interesting again is the future.

minutes I'll be out cold. And it looks like you'll have to nurse me for a while. You promise to do that?'

"'Of course,' replied Mrs. Monroe, eager to be let off the hook of food contamination, and he was quickly shown to the cool basement room with half-finished walls covered with simulated wood grain particle board. There were also bookshelves bearing Mr. Monroe's bonspiel trophies and the toys belonging to the three daughters: an array of Snoopy plush toys, Jem dolls, Easy Bake ovens, and Nancy Drew mystery novels. And the bed Buck was given to sleep in was smallish – a child's bed – covered with ruffled pink Fortrel sheets that smelled like they'd been sitting in a Goodwill shop for years. On the headboard there were scuffed up Holly Hobby, Veronica Lodge, and Betty Cooper stickers that had been stuck and halfheartedly peeled away. The room was obviously never used and pretty well forgotten, but Buck didn't mind. All he wanted to do was fall into a deep deep sleep. And so he did.

"Now, as you can imagine, the Monroe daughters were most excited indeed at having an astronaut/monster hibernating in their guest room. One by one the three daughters, Arleen, Darleen, and Serena came down to the room to stare at Buck, now sleeping in their old bed amid the clutter of their childhood. Mrs. Monroe wouldn't let her daughters peek long, still being fractionally convinced of her implication in Buck's illness, and shooed them away, wanting him to get better.

"Anyhow, life returned more or less to normal. Darleen and Serena went to work at the perfume counter of the local dime store, Mrs. Monroe's aloe product business picked up a bit, taking her out of the house, Mr. Monroe was out on his thresher, leaving only Arleen, the eldest daughter, who had recently been fired from the 7-Eleven, to take care of Buck.

"'Make sure he gets lots to eat!' shouted Mrs. Monroe from her salt-rusted blue Bonneville sedan as she screeched out of the driveway, to which Arleen waved and then rushed inside to the bathroom where she brushed her blonde feathered hair, applied alluring cosmetics, and then dashed down to the kitchen to whip up a special lunchtime treat for Buck, who, owing to his space poisoning, would only awaken once a day at noon, and then only for a half-hour. She made a platter of Vienna franks appended to toothpicks and accessorized by little blocks of orange cheese. These she prettily arranged on a platter in a shape reminiscent of the local shopping mall logo, the Crestwood Mall letter C, angled heavily to the right. *'Facing the future'* as the local newspaper had phrased it upon the mall's opening several hundred years previously when it was still 1974, even back then, since, as I have said, it has *al*ways been 1974 in Texlahoma. As far back as records go. Shopping malls, for instance, a recent innovation on Earth, have been supplying Texlahomans with running shoes, brass knickknacks, and whimsical greeting cards for untold millennia.

"Anyway, Arleen raced down to the basement with the food platter and pulled a chair up to the bed and pretended to read a book. When Buck woke up at one second past noon, the first thing he glimpsed was her reading, and he thought she looked ideal. As for Arleen, well, her heart had a romantic little arrhythmia right on the spot, even in spite of Buck's looking like a Frankenstein monster.

"'I'm hungry,' Buck said to Arleen, to which she replied, 'Won't you please please have some of these Vienna frank-and-cheese kebabs. I made them myself. They were most popular indeed at Uncle Clem's wake last year.'

"'Wake?' asked Buck.

"'Oh, yes. His combine overturned during the harvest, and he was trapped inside for two hours while he waited for the jaws of life to arrive. He wrote his will out in blood on the cab ceiling.'

"From that moment on, a conversational rapport developed between the two, and before long, love bloomed, but there was a problem with their love, for Buck would always fall back asleep almost as soon as he would awaken, owing to his space poisoning. This grieved Arleen.

"Finally one noon, just as Buck awoke, he said to Arleen, 'Arleen, I love you very much. Do you love *me*?' And, of course, Arleen replied, 'yes,' to which Buck said, 'Would you be willing to take a big risk and help me? We could be together always and I could help you leave Texlahoma. '

"Arleen was thrilled at both thoughts and said, 'Yes, yes,' and then Buck told her what she would have to do. Apparently, the radiation waves emitted by a woman in love are of just the right frequency to boost the rocket ship's engines and help it to lift off. And if Arleen would just come with him in the ship, they could leave, and Buck could get a cure for his space poisoning at the moon base. 'Will you help me, Arleen?'

"'Of course, Buck.'

"'There's just *one* catch.'

"'Oh?' Arleen froze.

"'You see, once we take off, there's only enough air in the ship for one person, and I'm afraid that after takeoff, you'd have to die. Sorry. But, of course, once we got to the moon, I'd have the right machines to revive you. There's really no problem.'

"Arleen stared at Buck, and a tear came down her cheek, dripped over her lip and onto her tongue, where it tasted salty, like urine. 'I'm sorry, Buck, but I can't do that,' she said, adding that things would probably be for the best if she no longer took care of him. Heartbroken but unsurprised, Buck fell back to sleep and Arleen went upstairs.

"Fortunately, Darleen, the youngest daughter, got fired from her perfume sales job that day and was able to take care of Buck next, while Arleen got hired at a fried chicken outlet and was no longer around to cast gloomy feelings on Buck.

"But with Buck's being on the rebound and Darleen's having too much free time on her hands, it was only a matter of minutes, practically, before love again blossomed. Days later, Buck was making the same plea for help to Darleen that he had made to Arleen, 'Won't you please help me, Darleen, I love you so much?'

"But when Buck's plea came to the part about Darleen's having to die, like her sister before her, she froze. 'I'm sorry, Buck, but I can't do that,' she, too, said, adding that things would probably be for the best if she no longer took care of him. Again heartbroken but again unsurprised, Buck fell back to sleep and Darleen went upstairs.

"Need I say it, but history repeated itself *again*. Darleen got hired at the local roadside steak house, and Serena, the middle child, got fired from Woolworth's scent counter and so was put in charge of taking care of Buck, who had ceased being a novelty in the basement and had become instead, kind of a grudge – of the same caliber of grudge as, say, a pet dog that the children argue over whose turn it is to feed. And when Serena appeared at noon with lunch one day, all Buck could bring himself to say was, 'God, did *another* one of you Monroe girls get fired? Can't any of you hold a job?'

"This just bounced right off of Serena. 'They're just small jobs,' she said. 'I'm learning how to paint and one of these days I'm going to become so good that Mr. Leo Castelli of the Leo Castelli art galleries of New York City is going to send a rescue party up to get me off of this God-forsaken asteroid. Here,' she said, jabbing a plate of crudité celery and carrot in his chest, 'eat these celery sticks and shut up. You look like you need fiber.'

"Well. If Buck thought he had been in love before, he realized now that those were merely mirages and that Serena was indeed his real True Love. He spent his waking time for the next few weeks savoring his half-hours which he spent telling Serena of the views of the heavens as seen from outer space, and listening to Serena talk of how she would paint the planets if only she could see what they looked like.

"'I can show you the heavens, and I can help you leave Texlahoma, too – if you're willing to come with me, Serena my love,' said Buck, who outlined his escape plans. And when he explained that Serena would have to die, she simply said, 'I understand.'

"The next day at noon when Buck awoke, Serena lifted him out of the bed and carried him out of the basement and up the stairs, where his feet knocked down framed family portraits taken years and years ago. 'Don't stop,' said Buck. 'Keep moving – we're running out of time.'

"It was a cold gray afternoon outside as Serena carried Buck across the yellowed autumn lawn and into the spaceship. Once inside, they sat down, closed the doors, and Buck used his last energies to turn the ignition and kiss Serena. True to his word, the love waves from her heart boosted the engine, and the ship took off, high into the sky and out of the gravitational field of Texlahoma. And before Serena passed out and then died from a lack of oxygen, the last sights she got to see were Buck's face shedding its pale green Frankenstein skin in lizardy chunks onto the dashboard, thus revealing the dashing pink young astronaut beneath, and outside she saw the glistening pale blue marble of Earth against the black heavens that the stars had stained like spilled milk.

"Below on Texlahoma, Arleen and Darleen, meanwhile, were both returning home from their jobs, from which they had both been fired, just in time to see the rocket fire off and their sister vanish into the stratosphere in a long, colonic, and fading white line. They sat on the swing set, unable to go back into the house, thinking and staring at the point where the jet's trail became nothing, listening to the creak of chains and the prairie wind.

"'You realize,' said Arleen, 'that that whole business of Buck being able to bring us back to life was total horseshit.'

"'Oh, I knew *that*,' said Darleen. 'But it doesn't change the fact that I feel jealous.'

"'No, it doesn't, does it?'

"And together the two sisters sat into the night, silhouetted by the luminescing Earth, having a contest with each other to see who could swing their swing the highest."

RE
CON
STRUCT

Claire and I never fell in love, even though we both tried hard. It happens. Anyhow, this is probably as good a point as any to tell something about myself. How shall I begin? Well, my name is Andrew Palmer, I'm almost thirty, I study languages (Japanese is my specialty), I come from a big family (more on that later), and I was born with an ectomorphic body, all skin and bones. However, after being inspired by a passage from the diaries of the Pop artist Mr. Andy Warhol – a passage where he expresses his sorrow after learning in his middle-fifties that if he had exercised, he could have had a body (imagine not having a body!) – I was galvanized into action. I began a dreary exercise regimen that turned my birdcage of a thorax into a pigeon breast. Hence, I now have a body – that's *one* problem out of the way. ¶But then, as mentioned, I've never been in love, and *that's* a problem. I just seem to end up as *friends* with everyone, and I tell you, I really hate it. I want to fall in love. ¶Or at least I think I do. ¶I'm not sure. It looks so . . . *messy*. ¶All right, all right, I *do* at least recognize the fact that I *don't* want to go through life alone, and to illustrate this, I'll tell you a secret story, a story I won't even tell Dag and Claire today out here on our desert picnic. It goes like this:

Once upon a time there was a young man named Edward who lived by himself with a great amount of dignity. He had so much dignity that when he made his solitary evening meal every night at six thirty, he always made sure he garnished it with a jaunty little sprig of parsley. That's how he thought the parsley looked: *jaunty*. Jaunty and dignified. He also made sure that he promptly washed *and* dried his dishes after completing his solitary evening meal. Only *lonely* people didn't take pride in their dinners and in their washing up, and Edward held it as a point of honor that while he had no need for people in his life, he was not going to be lonely. Life might not be much *fun*, mind you, but it seemed to have fewer people in it to irritate him.

Then one day Edward stopped drying the dishes and had a beer instead. Just for kicks. Just to relax. Then soon, the parsley disappeared from his dinners and another beer appeared. He made small excuses for it. I forget what they were.

Before long, dinner became the lonely *klonk* of a frozen dinner on the microwave floor saluted by the tinkle of Scotch and ice in a highball glass. Poor Edward was getting fed up with cooking and eating by himself, and before long, Edward's dinner became whatever he could microwave from the local Circle K nuke 'n' serve boutique – a beef-and-bean burrito, say, washed down with Polish cherry brandy, the taste for which he acquired during a long, sleepy earnest summer job

---

Bambification: The mental conversion of flesh-and-blood living creatures into cartoon characters possessing bourgeois Judeo-Christian attitudes and morals.

Diseases for Kisses (Hyperkarma): A deeply rooted belief that punishment will somehow always be far greater than the crime: ozone holes for littering.

spent behind the glum, patronless counter of the local Enver Hoxha Communist bookstore.

But even *then*, Edward found cooking and eating too much of a hassle, and dinner ended up becoming a glass of milk mixed in with whatever was in the discount bins at Liquor Barn. He began to forget what it felt like to pass firm stools and fantasized that he had diamonds in his eyes.

Again: poor Edward – his life seemed to be losing its *controlability*. One night, for instance, Edward was at a party in Canada but woke up the next morning in the United States, a two-hour drive away, and he couldn't even remember driving home or crossing the border.

Now, here's what Edward thought: he thought that he was a very smart guy in some ways. He had been to school, and he knew a great number of words. He could tell you that a *veronica* was a filmy piece of gossamer used to wrap the face of Jesus, or that a *cade* was a lamb abandoned by its mother and raised by human beings. Words, words, *words*.

Edward imagined that he was using these words to create his own private world – a magic and handsome room that only *he* could inhabit – a room in the proportion of a double cube, as defined by the British architect Adam. This room could only be entered through darkly stained doors that were padded with leather and horsehair that muffled the knocking of anyone who tried to enter and possibly disturb Edward's concentration.

In this room he had spent ten endless years. Large sections of its walls were lined with oak bookshelves, overflowing with volumes; framed maps covered other sections of walls that were painted the sapphire color of deep deep swimming pools. Imperial blue oriental carpets layered all of the floor and were frosted with the shed ivory hairs of Edward's trusty and faithful spaniel, Ludwig, who followed Edward everywhere. Ludwig would loyally listen to all Edward's piquant little observations on life, which he found himself not infrequently making while seated at his desk much of the day. At this desk he would also read and smoke a calabash pipe, while gazing out through leaded windows over a landscape that was forever a rainy fall afternoon in Scotland.

Of course, visitors were forbidden in this magic room, and only a Mrs. York was allowed in to bring him his rations – a bun-headed and betweeded grandmother, handcarved by central casting, who would deliver to Edward his daily (what else) cherry brandy, or, as time wore on, a forty-ounce bottle of Jack Daniels and a glass of milk.

Yes, Edward's was a sophisticated room, sometimes *so* sophisticated that it was only allowed to exist in black and white, reminiscent of an old drawing-room comedy. How's *that* for elegance?

So. What happened?

One day Edward was up on his wheeled bookshelf ladder and reaching for an old book he wanted to reread, in an attempt to take his mind off his concern that Mrs. York was late with his day's drink. But when he stepped down from the ladder, his feet went smack into a mound of Ludwig's dog mess and he got *very* angry. He walked toward the satin *chaise longue* behind which Ludwig was napping. "Ludwig," he shouted, "You *bad* dog, you. . . ."

But Edward didn't get far, for behind the sofa Ludwig had magically and (believe me) unexpectedly turned from a spunky, affectionate little funmoppet with an optimistically jittery little stub of tail into a flaring, black-gummed sepia gloss Rottweiler that pounced at Edward's throat, missing the jugular vein by a hair as Edward recoiled in horror. The new Ludwig-cum-Cerberus then went for Edward's shins with foaming fangs and the desperate wrenched offal howl of a dozen dogs being run over by trucks on the freeway.

Edward hopped epileptically onto the ladder and hollered for Mrs. York who, as fate would have it, he noticed just then out the window. She was wearing a blonde wig and a terry cloth robe and hopping into the little red sports car of a tennis pro, abandoning Edward's service forever. She looked quite smashing – dramatically lit under a harsh new sky that was scorching and ozoneless – *certainly* not at all an autumn sky in Scotland.

Well.

Poor Edward.

He was trapped in the room, able only to roll back and forth across the bookshelves on the heights of his wheeled ladder. Life in his once charmed room had become profoundly dreadful. The thermostat was out of reach and the air became muggy, fetid and Calcuttan. And of course, with Mrs. York gone, so were the cocktails to make this situation bearable.

Meanwhile, millipedes and earwigs, long asleep behind obscure top-shelf books, were awakened by Edward as he grimly reached for volumes to throw at Ludwig in an attempt to keep the monster at bay – from continually lunging at his pale trembling toes. These insects would crawl over Edward's hands. And books thrown at Ludwig would bounce insouciantly off his back, with the resulting pepper-colored shimmy of bugs that sprinkled onto the carpet being lapped up by Ludwig with his long pink tongue.

Edward's situation was indeed dire.

There was only one option of course, and that was to leave the room, and so, to the enraged thwarted howls of Ludwig who charged at Edward from across the room, Edward breathlessly opened his heavy oak doors, his tongue galvanized with the ferric taste of adrenalin, and, frantic but sad, left his once magic room for the first time in what seemed ever.

Ever was actually about ten years, and the sight Edward found outside those doors really amazed him. In all the time he had been sequestering himself, being piquant in his little room, the *rest* of humanity had been busy building something else – a vast city, built not of words but of relationships. A shimmering, endless New York, shaped of lipsticks, artillery shells, wedding cakes, and folded shirt cardboards; a city built of iron, papier-mâché and playing cards; an ugly/lovely world surfaced with carbon and icicles and bougainvillea vines. Its boulevards were patternless, helter-skelter, and cuckoo.

Spectacularism: A fascination with extreme situations.

Everywhere there were booby traps of mousetraps, Triffids, and black holes. And yet in spite of this city's transfixing madness, Edward noticed that its multitude of inhabitants moved about with ease, unconcerned that around any corner there might lurk a clown-tossed marshmallow cream pie, a *Brigada Rosa* kneecapping, or a kiss from the lovely film star Sophia Loren. And directions were impossible. But when he asked an inhabitant where he could buy a map, the inhabitant looked at Edward as though he were mad, then ran away screaming.

So Edward had to acknowledge that he was a country bumpkin in this Big City. He realized he had to learn all the ropes with a ten-year handicap, and that prospect was daunting. But then, in the same way that bumpkins vow to succeed in a new city because they know they have a fresh perspective, so vowed Edward.

And he promised that once he made his way in this world (without getting scalded to death by its many fountains of burning perfume or maimed by the endless truckloads of angry clucking cartoon chickens that were driven about the city's streets) he would build the tallest tower of them all. This silver tower would stand as a beacon to all voyagers who, like himself, arrived in the city late in life. And at the tower's peak there would be a rooftop patio lounge. In this lounge, Edward knew that he would do three things: he would serve tomato juice cocktails with little wedges of lemon, he would play jazz on a piano layered with zinc sheeting and photos of forgotten pop stars, and he would have a little pink booth, out back near the latrines, that sold (among other things) maps.

ENTER
HYPERSPACE

"Andy." Dag prods me with a greasy chicken bone, bringing me back to the picnic. "Stop being so quiet. It's your turn to tell a story, and do me a favor, babe – give me a dose of celebrity content." ¶*"Do* amuse us, darling," adds Claire. "You're being *so* moody." ¶Torpor defines my mood as I sit on the crumbling, poxed, and leprous never-used macadam at the corner of Cottonwood and Sapphire avenues, thinking my stories to myself and crumbling pungent sprigs of sage in my fingers. "Well, my brother, Tyler, once shared an elevator with David Bowie." ¶"How many floors?" ¶"I don't know. All I remember is that Tyler had no idea what to say to him. So he said nothing." ¶"I have found," says Claire, "that in the absence of anything to talk about with celebrities, you can always say to them, 'Oh, Mr. Celebrity! I've got *all* your albums' – even if they're not musicians." ¶"Look—" says Dag, turning his head, "some people are actually *driving* down here." ¶A black Buick sedan filled with young Japanese tourists – a rarity in a valley visited mainly by Canadians and West Germans – floats down the hill, the first vehicle in all the time we've been having our picnic. ¶"They probably took the

Verbenia Street off ramp by mistake. I bet you anything they're looking for the cement dinosaurs up at the Cabazon truck stop," Dag says.

"Andy, you speak Japanese. Go talk to them," Claire says.

"That's a bit presumptuous. Let them stop and ask directions first," which, of course, they immediately do. I rise and go to talk into their electronically lowered window. Inside the sedan are two couples, roughly my age, immaculately (one might say *sterilely* as though they were entering a region of biohazard) dressed in summer funwear and wearing the reserved, please-don't-murder-me smile Japanese tourists in North America started adopting a few years ago. The expressions immediately put me on the defensive, make me feel angry at *their* presumption of *my* violence. And God only knows what they make of our motley quintet and our Okie transport sprawled with meal remains of mismatched dishes. A blue jeans ad come to life.

I speak English (why ruin their desert USA fantasy?) and in the ensuing convulsed pidgin of hand signals and they-went-*that*-aways, I discover that the Japanese *do* want to go visit the dinosaurs. And shortly, after garnering directions, they are off in a puff of dust and roadside debris, from which we see a camera emerge, out of the rear window. The camera is held backward by one hand and a finger on top of it snaps our photo, at which point Dag shouts, "Look! A camera! Bite the insides of your cheeks, quick. Get those cheekbones

---

Lessness: A philosophy whereby one reconciles oneself with diminishing expectations of material wealth: *"I've given up wanting to make a killing or be a bigshot. I just want to find happiness and maybe open up a little roadside cafe in Idaho."*

Status Substitution: Using an object with intellectual or fashionable cachet to substitute for an object that is merely pricey: *"Brian, you left your copy of Camus in your brother's BMW."*

happening!" Then, once the car is out of view, Dag then jumps in on *me*: "And *what*, may I ask, was with your Arnold the Yokel act?"

"*Andrew*. You speak lovely Japanese," adds Claire. "You could have given them such a thrill."

"It wasn't called for," I reply, remembering how much of a letdown it was for me when I was living in Japan and people tried to speak to me in English. "But it *did* remind me of a bedtime story for today."

"Pray tell."

And so, as my friends, gleaming of cocoa butter, lean back and absorb the sun's heat, I tell my tale:

"A few years ago I was working at this teenybopper magazine office in Japan – part of a half-year job exchange program with the university – when a strange thing happened to me one day."

"Wait," interrupts Dag. "This is a true story?"

"Yes."

"Okay."

"It was a Friday morning and I, being a dutiful foreign photo researcher, was on the phone to London. I was on deadline to get some photos from Depeche Mode's people who were at some house party there – an awful Eurosquawk was on the other end. My ear was glued to the receiver and my hand was over the other ear trying to block out the buzz of the office, a frantic casino of Ziggy Stardust coworkers with everyone hyper from ten-dollar Tokyo coffees from the shop across the street.

"I remember what was going through my mind, and it wasn't my job – it was the way that cities have their own signature odor to them. Tokyo's street smell put this into my mind – *udon* noodle broth and faint sewage; chocolate and car fumes. And I thought of Milan's smell – of cinnamon and diesel belch and roses – and Vancouver with its Chinese roast pork and salt water and cedar. I was feeling homesick for Portland, trying to remember its smell of trees and rust and moss when the ruckus of the office began to dim perceptibly.

"A tiny old man in a black Balmain suit came into the room. His skin was all folded like a shrunken apple-head person's, but it was dark, peat-colored, and shiny like an old baseball mitt or the Bog Man of Denmark. And he was wearing a baseball cap and chatting with my working superiors.

"Miss Ueno, the drop-dead cool fashion coordinator in the desk next to mine (Olive Oyl hair; Venetian gondolier's shirt; harem pants and Viva Las Vegas booties), became flustered the way a small child does when presented with a bear-sized boozed-up drunk uncle at the front door on a snowy winter night. I asked Miss Ueno who this guy was and she said it was Mr. Takamichi, the *kacho*, the Grand Poobah of the company, an Americaphile renowned for bragging about his golf scores in Parisian brothels and for jogging through Tasmanian gaming houses with an L.A. blonde on each arm.

"Miss Ueno looked really stressed. I asked her why. She said she wasn't stressed but angry. She was angry because no matter how hard she worked she was more or less stuck at her little desk forever – a cramped cluster of desks being the Japanese equivalent of the veal fattening pen. 'But not only because I'm a woman,' she said, 'but also because I'm a Japanese. *Mostly* because I'm a Japanese. I have ambition. In any other country I could rise, but here I just sit. I murder my ambition.' She said that Mr. Takamichi's appearance somehow simply underscored her situation. The hopelessness.

"At that point, Mr. Takamichi headed over to my desk. I just knew this was going to happen. It was really embarrassing. In Japan you get phobic about being singled out from the crowd. It's about the worst thing that someone can do to you.

"'You must be Andrew,' he said, and he shook my hands like a Ford dealer. 'Come on upstairs. We'll have drinks. We'll talk,' he said, and I could feel Miss Ueno burning like a road flare of resentment next to me. And so I introduced her, but Mr. Takamichi's response was benign. A grunt. Poor Japanese people. Poor Miss Ueno. She was right – they're just so trapped wherever they are – frozen on this awful boring ladder.

"And as we were walking toward the elevator, I could feel everyone in the office shooting jealousy rays at me. It was such a bad scene and I could just imagine everyone thinking 'who does he think he is?' I felt dishonest. Like I was coasting on my foreignness. I felt I was being excommunicated from the *shin jin rui* – that's what the Japanese newspapers call people like those kids in their twenties at the office – *new human beings*. It's hard to explain. We have the same group over here and it's just as large, but it doesn't have a name – an X generation – purposefully hiding itself. There's more space over here to hide in – to get lost in – to use as camouflage. You're not allowed to disappear in Japan.

"But I digress.

"We went upstairs in the elevator to a floor that required a special key for access, and Mr. Takamichi was being sort of theatrically ballsy the whole way up, like a cartoon version of an American, you know, talking about football and stuff. But once we got to the top he suddenly turned Japanese – so quiet. He turned right off – like I'd flipped a switch. I got really worried that I was going to have to endure three hours of talk about the weather.

"We walked down a thickly carpeted hallway, dead silent, past small Impressionist paintings and tufts of flowers arranged in vases in the Victorian style. This was the western part of his floor. And when this part ended, we came to the Japanese part. It was like entering hyperspace, at which point Mr. Takamichi pointed to a navy cotton robe for me to change into, which I did.

"Inside the main Japanese room that we entered there was a *toko no ma* shrine with chrysanthemums, a scroll, and a gold fan. And in the center of the room was a low black table surrounded by terra-cotta colored cushions. On the table were two onyx carp and settings for tea.

The one artifact in the room that jarred was a small safe placed in a corner – not even a good safe, mind you, but an inexpensive model of the sort that you might have expected to find in the back office of a Lincoln, Nebraska shoe store just after World War II – really cheap looking, and in gross contrast to the rest of the room.

"Mr. Takamichi asked me to sit down at the table whereupon we sat down for salty green Japanese tea.

"Of course, I was wondering what his hidden agenda was in getting me up into his room. He talked pleasantly enough . . . how did I like my job? . . . what did I think of Japan? . . . stories about his kids. Nice boring stuff. And he told a few stories about time he had spent in New York in the 1950s as a stringer for the *Asahi* newspapers . . . about meeting Diana Vreeland and Truman Capote and Judy Holiday. And after a half-hour or so, we shifted to warmed sake, delivered, with the clapping of Mr. Takamichi's hands, by a midge of a servant in a drab brown kimono the color of shopping-bag paper.

"And after the servant left, there was a pause. It was then that he asked me what I thought the most valuable *thing* was that I owned.

"Well, well. The most valuable *thing* that I owned. Try and explain the concept of sophomoric minimalism to an octogenarian Japanese publishing magnate. It's not easy. What thing could you possibly own of any value? I mean *really*. A beat up VW Bug? A stereo? I'd sooner have died than admit that the most valuable *thing* I owned was a fairly extensive collection of German industrial music dance mix EP records stored, for even further embarrassment, under a box of crumbling Christmas tree ornaments in a Portland, Oregon basement. So I said, quite truthfully (and, it dawned on me, quite re*fresh*ingly), that I owned no *thing* of any value.

He then changed the discussion to the necessity of wealth being transportable, being converted into paintings, gems, and precious metals and so forth (he'd been through wars and the depression and spoke with authority), but I'd pushed some right button, said the right thing – passed a test – and his tone of voice was pleased. Then, maybe ten minutes later, he clapped his hands again, and the tiny servant in the noiseless brown kimono reappeared and was barked an instruction. This caused the servant to go to the corner and to roll the cheap little safe across the tatami mat floor next to where Mr. Takamichi sat cross-legged on the cushions.

"Then, looking hesitant but relaxed, he dialed his combination on the knob. There was a click, he pulled a bar, and the door opened, revealing *what*, I couldn't see.

"He reached in and pulled out what I could tell to be from the distance, a photograph – a black-and-white 1950s photo, like the shots they take at the scene of the crime. He looked at the mystery picture and sighed. Then, flipping it over and giving it to me with a little outpuff of breath meaning 'this is *my* most valuable thing,' he handed me the photo and I was, I'll admit, shocked at what it was.

"It was a photo of Marilyn Monroe getting into a Checker cab, lifting up her dress, no underwear, and smooching at the photographer, presumably Mr. Takamichi in his stringer days. It was an unabashedly sexual frontal photo (get your minds out of the gutter – black as the ace of spades, if you must know) and very taunting. Looking at it, I said to Mr. Takamichi, who was waiting expressionlessly for a reaction, "Well, well," or some such drivel, but internally I was actually quite mortified that this photo, essentially only a cheesy paparazzi shot, unpublishable at that, was his most valued possession.

"And then I had an uncontrollable reaction. Blood rushed to my ears, and my heart went bang; I broke out into a sweat and the words of Rilke, the poet, entered my brain – his notion that we are all of us born with a letter inside us, and that only if we are true to ourselves, may we be allowed to read it before we die. The burning blood in my ears told me that Mr. Takamichi had somehow mistaken the Monroe photo in the safe for the letter inside of himself, and that I, myself, was in peril of making some sort of similar mistake.

"I smiled pleasantly enough, I hope, but I was reaching for my pants and making excuses, blind, grabbing excuses, while I raced to the elevator, buttoning up my shirt and bowing along the way to the confused audience of Mr. Takamichi hobbling behind me making old man noises. Maybe he thought I'd be excited by his photo or complimentary or aroused even, but I don't think he expected rudeness. The poor guy.

"But what's done is done. There is no shame in impulse. Breathing stertorously, as though I had just vandalized a house, I fled the building, without even collecting my things – just like you, Dag – and that night I packed my bags. On the plane a day later, I thought of more Rilke:

Only the individual who is solitary is like a thing subject to profound laws, and if he goes out into the morning that is just beginning, or looks out into the evening that is full of things happening, and if he feels what is going on there, then his whole situation drops from him as from a dead man, although he stands in the very midst of life.

"Two days later I was back in Oregon, back in the New World, breathing less crowded airs, but I knew even then that there was still too much history there for me. That I needed *less* in life. Less past.

"So I came down here, to breathe dust and walk with the dogs – to look at a rock or a cactus and know that I am the first person to see that cactus and that rock. And to try and read the letter inside me."

DECEMBER 31, 1999

For the record, just as happened with me, Dag and Claire never fell in love, either. I guess that would just be too easy. Instead, they became pals, too, and I must say, if nothing else, all of us just being friends *does* simplify life. ¶There was a weekend about eight months ago when a flock of Baxters, dressed in neon colors and flaps and pouches and zippers – like a teeny little rock video – appeared from Los Angeles to grill myself and Dag about our relationship with Claire. I remember brother Allan, the frat boy, telling me in my kitchen, while Claire and others were sitting by my fire, that at that very moment another Baxter sibling was in Claire's bungalow checking her bedsheets for strange hairs. What a horrible, nosy, prudish family even in spite of their hipness, and no wonder Claire wanted to get away from them. "Come on, Spinster," demanded Allan, "guys just aren't friends with girls." ¶I mention this simply because I would like to point out that while I was telling my Japanese story, Claire was rubbing Dag's neck and that this gesture was entirely platonic. And at the end of my story, Claire clapped her hands, told Dag it was his turn for a story, and then came over and sat in front of me, requesting to have her back rubbed – it was just as platonic, too. Easy.

"I've got an end-of-the-world story," says Dag, finishing off the remainder of the iced tea, ice cubes long melted. He then takes off his shirt, revealing his somewhat ribby chest, lights another filter-tipped cigarette, and clears his throat in a nervous gesture.

The end of the world is a recurring motif in Dag's bedtime stories, eschatological You-Are-There accounts of what it's like to be Bombed, lovingly detailed, and told in deadpan voice. And so, with little more ado, he begins:

"Imagine you're standing in line at a supermarket, say, the Vons supermarket at the corner of Sunset and Tahquitz – but theoretically it can be any supermarket anywhere – and you're in just a vile mood because driving over you got into an argument with your best friend. The argument started over a road sign saying Deer Next 2 Miles and you said, 'Oh, *really*, they expect us to believe there are any deer left?' which made your best friend, who was sitting in the passenger seat looking through the box of cassette tapes, curl up their toes inside their running shoes. And you sense you've said something that's struck a nerve and it was fun, so you pushed things further: 'For that matter,' you said, 'you don't see nearly as many *birds* these days as you used to, do you? *And*, you know what I heard the other day? That down in the Caribbean, there aren't

any shells left anywhere because the tourists took them all. *And*, haven't you ever wondered when flying back from Europe, five miles over Greenland, that there's just something, I don't know – *inverted* – about shopping for cameras and Scotch and cigarettes up in outer space?'

"Your friend then exploded, called you a real dink, and said, 'Why the hell are you so negative all the time? Do you have to see something depressing in everything?'

"You said back, 'Negative? *Moi?* I think realistic might be a better word. You mean to tell me we can drive all the way here from L.A. and see maybe ten thousand square miles of shopping malls, and you don't have maybe just the *weentsiest* inkling that something, somewhere, has gone *very very* cuckoo?'

"The whole argument goes nowhere, of course. That sort of argument always does, and possibly you are accused of being unfashionably negative. The net result is you standing alone in Vons checkout line number three with marshmallows and briquettes for the evening barbecue, a stomach that's quilted and acidic with pissed-offedness, and your best friend sitting out in the car, pointedly avoiding you and sulkily listening to big band music on the A.M. radio station that broadcasts ice rink music down valley from Cathedral City.

"But a part of you is also fascinated with the cart contents of the by-any-standards-obese man in line up ahead of you.

"My gosh, he's got one of everything in there! Plastic magnums of diet colas, butterscotch-flavored microwave cake mixes complete with their own baking tins (ten minutes of convenience; ten million years in the Riverside County

---

Survivulousness: The tendency to visualize oneself enjoying being the last remaining person on Earth. *"I'd take a helicopter up and throw microwave ovens down on the Taco Bell."*

Platonic Shadow: A nonsexual friendship with a member of the opposite sex.

Municipal Sanitary Landfill), and gallons and gallons of bottled spaghetti sauce . . . why his whole family must be awfully constipated with a diet like that, and hey – isn't that a *goiter* on his neck? 'Gosh, the price of milk is *so* cheap, these days,' you say to yourself, noting a price tag on one of his bottles. You smell the sweet cherry odor of the gum rack and unread magazines, cheap and alluring.

"But suddenly there's a power surge.

"The lights brighten, return to normal, dim, then die. Next to go is the Muzak, followed by a rising buzz of conversation similar to that in a movie theater when a film snaps. Already people are heading to aisle seven to grab the candles.

"By the exit, an elderly shopper is peevishly trying to bash her cart through electric doors that won't open. A staff member is trying to explain that the power is out. Through the other exit, propped open by a shopping cart, you see your best friend enter the store. 'The radio died,' your friend announces, 'and look –' out the front windows you see scores of vapor trails exiting the direction of the Twentynine Palms Marine base up the valley, '– something big's going on.'

"That's when the sirens begin, the worst sound in the world, and the sound you've dreaded all your life. It's *here*: the soundtrack to hell – wailing, flaring, warbling, and unreal – collapsing and confusing both time and space the way an ex-smoker collapses time and space at night when they dream in horror that they find themselves smoking. But here the ex-smoker wakes up to find a lit cigarette in his hand and the horror is complete.

"The manager is heard through a bullhorn, asking shoppers to calmly vacate, but no one's paying much attention. Carts are left in the aisles and the bodies flee, carrying and dropping looted roast beefs and bottles of Evian on the sidewalk outside.

Mental Ground Zero: The location where one visualizes oneself during the dropping of the atomic bomb; frequently, a shopping mall.

The parking lot is now about as civilized as a theme park's bumper cars.

"But the fat man remains, as does the cashier, who is wispily blonde, with a bony hillbilly nose and translucent white skin. They, your best friend, and you remain frozen, speechless, and your minds become the backlit NORAD world map of mythology – how cliché! And on it are the traced paths of fireballs, stealthily, inexorably passing over Baffin Island, the Aleutians, Labrador, the Azores, Lake Superior, the Queen Charlotte Islands, Puget Sound, Maine . . . it's only a matter of moments now, isn't it?

"'I always promised myself,' says the fat man, in a voice so normal as to cause the three of you to be jolted out of your thoughts, 'that when this moment came, I would behave with some dignity in whatever time remains and so, Miss –' he says, turning to the clerk in particular, 'let me please pay for my purchases.' The clerk, in the absence of other choices, accepts his money.

"Then comes The Flash.

"'Get down,' you shout, but they continue their transaction, deer transfixed by headlights. 'There's no time!' But your warning remains unheeded.

"And so then, *just* before the front windows become a crinkled, liquefied imploding sheet – the surface of a swimming pool during a high dive, as seen from below –

"– And *just* before you're pelleted by a hail of gum and magazines –

"– And *just* before the fat man is lifted off his feet, hung in suspended animation and bursts into flames while the liquefied ceiling lifts and drips upward –

"*Just* before all of this, your best friend cranes his neck, lurches over to where you lie, and kisses you on the mouth, after which he says to you, 'There. I've always wanted to do that.'

"And that's that. In the silent rush of hot wind, like the opening of a trillion oven doors that you've been imagining since you were six, it's all over: kind of scary, kind of sexy, and tainted by regret. A lot like life, wouldn't you say?"

PART TWO

NEW ZEALAND
GETS NUKED,
TOO

Five days ago – the day after our picnic – Dag disappeared. Otherwise the week has been normal, with myself and Claire slogging away at our McJobs – me tending bar at Larry's and maintaining the bungalows (I get reduced rent in return for minor caretaking) and Claire peddling five-thousand-dollar purses to old bags. ¶Of course we wonder where Dag went, but we're not too worried. He's obviously just Dagged-out someplace, possibly crossing the border at Mexicali and off to write heroic couplets out among the saguaro, or maybe he's in L.A., learning about CAD systems or making a black-and-white super-8 movie. Brief creative bursts that allow him to endure the tedium of real work. ¶And this is fine. ¶But I wish he'd given some advance notice so I wouldn't have to knock myself out covering his tail for him at work. He knows that Mr. MacArthur, the bar's owner and our boss, lets him get away with murder. He'll make one quick joke, and his absence will be forgotten. Like the last time: ¶"Won't happen again, Mr. M. By the way, how many lesbians does it take to put in a light bulb?" ¶Mr. MacArthur winces. "Dagmar, *shhh!* For God's sake, don't irritate the clientele!" On certain nights of the week

Larry's can have its share of stool-throwing aficionados. Bar brawls, although colorful, only up Mr. M.'s Allstate premiums. Not that I've ever seen a brawl at Larry's. Mr. M. is merely paranoid.

"Three – one to put in the light bulb and two to make a documentary about it."

Forced laughter; I don't think he got it. "Dagmar, you are very funny, but please don't upset the ladies."

"But, Mr. MacArthur," says Dag, repeating his personal tag line, "I'm a lesbian myself. I just happen to be trapped in a man's body."

This, of course, is an overload for Mr. M., product of another era, a depression child and owner of a sizable collection of matchbook folders from Waikiki, Boca Raton, and Gatwick Airport; Mr. MacArthur who, with his wife, clips coupons, shops in bulk, and fails to understand the concept of moist microheated terry towels given before meals on airline flights. Dag once tried to explain "the terry-towel concept" to Mr. M.: "Another ploy dreamed up by the marketing department, you know – let the peons wipe the ink of thriller and romance novels from their fingers before digging into the grub. *Très* swank. Wows the yokels." But Dag, for all of his efforts, might as well have been talking to a cat. Our parents' generation seems neither able nor interested in understanding how marketers exploit them. They take shopping at face value.

But life goes on.

Where are you, Dag?

Dag's been found! He's in (of all places) Scotty's Junction, Nevada, just east of the Mojave Desert. He telephoned: "You'd love it here, Andy. Scotty's Junction is where atom bomb scientists, mad with grief over their spawn, would come and get sloshed in the Ford saloon cars in which they'd then crash and burn in the ravines; afterward, the little desert animals came and ate them. So tasty. So *bib*lical. I *love* desert justice."

"You dink. I've been working double shift because of your leaving unannounced."

"I had to go, Andy. Sorry if I left you in the lurch."

"Dag, what the *hell* are you doing in Nevada?"

"You wouldn't understand."

"Try me."

"I don't know—"

"Then make a *story* out of it. Where are you calling from?"

"I'm inside a diner at a pay phone. I'm using Mr. M.'s calling card number. He won't mind."

"You really abuse that guy's goodwill, Dag. You can't coast on your charm forever."

"Did I phone Dial-a-Lecture? And do you want to hear my story or not?"

Of course I do. "Okay, so I'll shut up, already. Shoot."

I hear gas station dings in the background, along with *skree*ing wind, audible even from inside. The unbeautiful desolation of Nevada already makes me feel lonely; I pull my shirt up around my neck to combat a shiver.

Dag's roadside diner smells, no doubt, like a stale bar carpet. Ugly people with eleven fingers are playing computer slots built into the counter and eating greasy meat byproducts slathered in cheerfully tinted condiments. There's a cold, humid mist, smelling of cheap floor cleaner, mongrel dog, cigarettes, mashed potato, and failure. And the patrons are staring at Dag, watching him contort and die romantically into the phone with his tales of tragedy and probably wondering as they view his dirty white shirt, askew tie, and jittery cigarette, whether a posse of robust, clean-suited Mormons will burst in the door at any moment, rope him with a long white lasso, and wrestle him back across the Utah state line.

"Here's the story, Andy, and I'll try and be fast, so here goes: once upon a time there was a young man who was living

---

Cult of Aloneness: The need for autonomy at all costs, usually at the expense of long-term relationships. Often brought about by overly high expectations of others.

in Palm Springs and minding his own business. We'll call him Otis. Otis had moved to Palm Springs because he had studied weather charts and he knew that it received a ridiculously small amount of rain. Thus he knew that if the city of Los Angeles over the mountain was ever beaned by a nuclear strike, wind currents would almost entirely prevent fallout from reaching his lungs. Palm Springs was his own personal New Zealand; a sanctuary. Like a surprisingly large number of people, Otis thought a lot about New Zealand and the Bomb.

"One day in the mail Otis received a postcard from an old friend who was now living in New Mexico, a two-day drive away. And what interested Otis about this card was the photo on the front – a 1960s picture of a daytime desert nuclear test shot, taken from a plane.

"The postcard got Otis to thinking.

"*Something* disturbed him about the photo, but he couldn't quite figure out *what*.

"Then Otis figured it out: the scale was wrong – the mushroom cloud was *too small*. Otis had always thought nuclear mushroom clouds occupied the *whole* sky, but this explosion, why, it was a teeny little road flare, lost out amid the valleys and mountain ranges in which it was detonated.

"Otis panicked.

"'Maybe,' he thought to himself, 'I've spent my whole life worrying about tiny little firecrackers made monstrous in our minds and on TV. Can I have been *wrong* all this time? Maybe I can free myself of Bomb anxiety –'

"Otis was excited. He realized he had no choice but to hop into his car, pronto, and investigate further – to visit *actual* test sites and figure out as best he could the size of an explosion. So he made a tour of what he called the Nuclear Road – southern Nevada, southwestern Utah, and then a loop down in to New Mexico to the test sites in Alamogordo and Las Cruces.

Celebrity Schadenfreude: Lurid thrills derived from talking about celebrity deaths.

"Otis made Las Vegas the first night. There he could have *sworn* he saw Jill St. John screaming at her cinnamon-colored wig floating in a fountain. And he *possibly* saw Sammy Davis, Jr. offer her a bowl of nuts in consolation. And when he hesitated in betting at a blackjack table, the guy next to him snarled, '*Hey, bub* (he actually got called "bub" – he was in heaven), *Vegas wasn't built on winners.*' Otis tossed the man a one-dollar gaming chip.

"The next morning on the highway Otis saw 18-wheel big rigs aimed at Mustang, Ely, and Susanville, armed with guns, uniforms, and beef, and before long he was in southwest Utah visiting the filming site of a John Wayne movie – the movie where more than half the people involved in its making died of cancer. Clearly, Otis's was an exciting drive – exciting but lonely.

"I'll spare the rest of Otis's trip, but you get the point. Most importantly, in a few days Otis found the bombed New Mexican moonscapes he was looking for and realized, after a thorough inspection, that his perception of earlier in the week was correct, that yes, *atomic bomb mushroom clouds really are much smaller than we make them out to be in our minds.* And he derived comfort from this realization – a silencing of the small whispering nuclear voices that had been speaking continually in his subconscious since kindergarten. There was nothing to worry about after all."

"So your story has a happy ending, then?"

"Not really, Andy. You see, Otis's comfort was short lived, for he soon after had a scary realization – a realization triggered by shopping malls, of all things. It happened this way: he was driving home to California on Interstate 10 and passing by a shopping mall outside of Phoenix. He was idly thinking about the vast, arrogant block forms of shopping mall architecture and how they make as little visual sense in the landscape as nuclear cooling towers. He then drove past a new yuppie housing development – one of those strange new developments with hundreds of blockish, equally senseless and enormous coral pink houses, all of them with an inch of space in between and located about three feet from the highway. And Otis got to thinking: 'Hey! these aren't houses at all – these are *malls in disguise*.'

"Otis developed the shopping mall correlation: kitchens became the Food Fair; living rooms the Fun Center; the bathroom the Water Park. Otis said to himself, 'God, what goes through the *minds* of people who live in these things – are they *shopping*?'

"He knew he was on to a hot and scary idea; he had to pull his car over to the side of the road to think while freeway cars slashed past.

"And that's when he lost his newly found sense of comfort. '*If* people can mentally convert their houses into shopping malls,' he thought, 'then these same people are just as capable of mentally equating atomic bombs with regular bombs.'

"He combined this with his new observation about mushroom clouds: 'And once these people saw the new, smaller *friendlier* explosion size, the conversion process would be irreversible. All vigilance would disappear. Why, before you knew

---

The Emperor's New Mall: The popular notion that shopping malls exist on the insides only and have no exterior. The suspension of visual belief engendered by this notion allows shoppers to pretend that the large, cement blocks thrust into their environment do not, in fact, exist.

it you'd be able to buy atomic bombs over the counter – or *free with a tank of gas!* Otis's world was scary once more."

"Was he on drugs?" asks Claire.

"Just coffee. Nine cups from the sound of it. Intense little guy."

"I think he thinks about getting blown up too much. I think he needs to fall in love. If he doesn't fall in love soon, he's really going to lose it."

"That may be. He's coming home tomorrow afternoon. He's got presents for both of us, he says."

"Pinch me."

MONSTERS
EXIST

Dag has just driven in and looks like something the doggies pulled out of the dumpsters of Cathedral City. His normally pink cheeks are a dove gray, and his chestnut hair has the demented mussed look of a random sniper poking his head out from a burger joint and yelling, "I'll never surrender." We can see all of this the moment he walks in the door – he's totally wired and he hasn't been sleeping. I'm concerned, and from the way Claire nervously changes her hold on her cigarette I can tell she's worried, too. Still, Dag looks happy, which is all anyone can ask for, but why does his happiness look so, so – suspicious ¶*I think I know why.* ¶I've seen this flavour of happiness before. It's of the same phylum of unregulated relief and despondent giggliness I've seen in the faces of friends returning from half-years spent in Europe – faces showing relief at being able to indulge in big cars, fluffy white towels, and California produce once more, but faces also gearing up for the inevitable "what-am-I-going-to-do-with-my-life?" semiclinical depression that almost always bookends a European pilgrimage. ¶*Uh oh.* ¶But then Dag's already *had* his big mid-twenties crisis, and thank God these things only happen once. So I guess he's just been alone for too many days – not having conversation with people makes you go nuts. It really does. Especially in Nevada.

"Hi, funsters! Treats for all," Dag yells to us, reeling through the door, carrying a paper loot sack across Claire's threshold, pausing briefly to snoop Claire's mail on the hall table, and allowing a fraction of a second for Claire and me to exchange a meaningful, raised-eyebrow glance as we sit on her couches playing Scrabble, and time enough also for her to whisper to me, "*Do* something."

"Hi, Cupcake," Claire then says, click-clicking across the wood floor on platform cork wedges and hamming it up in a flare-legged lavender toreador jumpsuit. "I dressed as a Reno housewife in your honor. I even attempted a beehive do, but I ran out of hairspray. So it kind of turned into a *don't*. Want a drink?"

"A vodka and orange would be nice. Hi, Andy."

"Hi, Dag," I say, getting up and walking past him, out the front door. "Gotta pee. Claire's loo is making funny sounds. See you in a second. Long drive today?"

"Twelve hours."

"Love ya."

Back across the courtyard in my clean but disorganized little bungalow, I dig through my bottom bathroom drawer and locate a prescription bottle left over from my fun-with-downers phase of a year or two ago. From the bottle I extract five orange 0.50 mg. Xanax brand tranquilizer tablets, wait for a pee-ish length of time, then return to Claire's, where I grind

---

Poorochondria: Hypochondria derived from not having medical insurance.

Personal Tabu: A small rule for living, bordering on a superstition, that allows one to cope with everyday life in the absence of cultural or religious dictums.

them up with her spice pestle, slipping the resultant powder into Dag's vodka and orange. "Well, Dag. You look like a rat's nest at the moment, but *hey*, here's to you, anyway." We toast (me with a soda), and after watching him down his drink, I realize in an electric guilt jolt in the back of my neck, that I've misdosed him – rather than having him simply relax a bit (as was intended), I now gave him about fifteen minutes before he turns into a piece of furniture. Best never to mention this to Claire.

"Dagmar, my gift please," Claire says, her voice contrived and synthetically perky, overcompensating for her concern about Dag's distress-sale condition.

"In good time, you lucky lucky children," Dag says, tottering on his seat, "in good time. I want to relax a second." We sip and take in Claire's pad. "Claire, your place is spotless and charming as usual."

"Gee, thanks Dag." Claire assumes Dag is being supercilious, but actually, Dag and I have always admired Claire's taste – her bungalow is quantum leaps in taste ahead of both of ours, furnished with heaps of familial loot snagged in between her mother's and father's plentiful Brentwood divorces.

Claire will go to incredible lengths to get the desired

**SEMI-DISPOSABLE
SWEDISH FURNITURE**

effects. ("My apartment must be *perfect*.") She pulled up the carpet, for instance, and revealed hardwood flooring, which she hand-refinished, stained, and then sprinkled with Persian and Mexican throw rugs. Antique plate silver jugs and vases (Orange County Flea Market) rest in front of walls covered with fabric. Outdoorsy Adirondack chairs made of cascara willow bear cushions of Provençal material printed by wood block.

Claire's is a lovely space, but it has one truly *disturbing* artifact in it – racks of antlers, dozens of them, lying tangled in a brittle calciferous cluster in the room adjoining the kitchen, the room that technically really *ought* to have been the dining room instead of an ossuary that scares the daylights out of repairpersons come to fix the appliances.

The antler-collecting obsession started months ago, when Claire "liberated" a rack of elk antlers from a nearby garage sale. A few days later she informed Dag and me that she had performed a small ceremony to allow the soul of the tortured, hunted animal to go to heaven. She wouldn't tell us what the ceremony was.

Soon, the liberation process became a small obsession. Claire now rescues antlers by placing ads in the *Desert Sun* saying, "Local artist requires antlers for project. Please call 323. . . ." Nine times out of ten the respondent is a woman named Verna, hair in curlers, chewing nicotine gum, who

---

Architectural Indigestion: The almost obsessive need to live in a "cool" architectural environment. Frequently related objects of fetish include framed black-and-white art photography (Diane Arbus a favorite); simplistic pine furniture; matte black high-tech items such as TVs, stereos, and telephones; low-wattage ambient lighting; a lamp, chair, or table that alludes to the 1950s; cut flowers with complex names.

Japanese Minimalism: The most frequently offered interior design aesthetic used by rootless career-hopping young people.

says to Claire, "You don't look the scrimshaw type to me, honey, but the bastard's gone, so just take the damn things. Never could stand them, anyway."

"Well, Dag," I ask, reaching for his paper bags, "what did you get me?"

"Hands off the merchandise, please!" Dag snaps, adding quickly, "Patience. Please." He then reaches into the bag and then hands me something quickly before I can see what it is. "*Un cadeau pour toi.*"

It's a coiled-up antique bead belt with GRAND CANYON written on it in bead-ese.

"Dag! This is perfect! Total 1940s."

"Thought you'd like it. And now for *mademoiselle* –" Dag pivots and hands Claire something: a de-labeled Miracle Whip mayonnaise jar filled with something green. "Possibly the most charmed object in my collection."

"*Mille tendresses*, Dag," Claire says, looking into what looks like olive-colored instant coffee crystals, "but what is it? Green sand?" She shows the jar to me, then shakes it a bit. "I *am* perplexed. Is it jade?"

"Not jade at all."

A sick shiver marimbas down my spine. "Dag, you didn't get it in New Mexico, did you?"

"Good guess, Andy. Then you know what it is?"

"I have a hunch."

"You kittenish thing, you."

"Will you two stop being so *male*, and just tell me what this stuff is?" demands Claire. "My cheeks are hurting from smiling."

I ask Claire if I can see her present for a second, and she hands me the jar, but Dag tries to grab it from me. I guess his cocktail is starting to kick in. "It's not really radioactive, is it, Dag?" I ask.

"Radioactive!" Claire shrieks. This scares Dag. He drops the jar and it shatters. Within moments, countless green glass beads explode like a cluster of angry hornets, shooting everywhere, rattling down the floor, rolling into cracks, into the couch fabric, into the ficus soil – *everywhere.*

"Dag, what is this shit? Clean it up! Get it out of my house!"

"It's Trinitite," mumbles Dag, more crestfallen than upset. "It's from Alamogordo, where they had the first N-test. The heat was so intense it melted the sand into a new substance altogether. I bought a bottle at a ladies' auxiliary clothing store."

"Oh my god. It's plutonium! You brought plutonium into my house. You are *such* an *ass*hole. This place is a waste dump now." She gathers breath. "I can't live here anymore! I have to move! My perfect little house – I live in a toxic waste dump –" Claire starts dancing the chicken in her wedgies, her pale face red with hysteria, yet making no guilt inroads on a rapidly fading Dag.

Stupidly I try to be the voice of reason: "Claire, come on. The explosion was almost fifty years ago. The stuff is harmless now –"

"*Then you can harmless it all right into the trash for me*, Mr. Know Everything. You don't actually believe all of that *harmless* talk, do you? You are *such* a victim, you pea-brained dimwit – no one believes the government. This stuff's *death* for the next four and a half billion years."

Dag mumbles a phrase from the couch, where he's almost asleep. "You're overreacting, Claire. The beads are half-lived out. They're clean."

"Don't even *speak to* me, you hell-bound P.R. Frankenstein monster, until you've decontaminated this entire house. Until then, I'll be staying at Andy's. Good *night.*"

She roars out the door like a runaway train car, leaving Dag near comatose on the couch, condemned to a sleep of febrile pale green nightmares. Claire may or may not have nightmares, but should she ever come back to this bungalow, she'll never be able to sleep there quite perfectly ever again.

Tobias arrives to visit Claire tomorrow. And Christmas with the family in Portland soon. Why is it so impossible to de-complicate my life?

DON'T
EAT
YOURSELF

An action-packed day. Dag is still asleep on Claire's sofa, unaware of how deeply he has plunged on her shit list. Claire, meanwhile, is in my bathroom, dolling herself up and philosophizing out loud through a steamy Givenchy-scented murk and amid a counterload of cosmetics and accessories I was made to fetch from her bungalow that resembles the emptied-out contents of a child's Halloween sack: ¶"Everybody has a 'gripping stranger' in their lives, Andy, a stranger who unwittingly possesses a bizarre hold over you. Maybe it's the kid in cut-offs who mows your lawn or the woman wearing White Shoulders who stamps your book at the library – a stranger who, if you were to come home and find a message from them on your answering machine saying, '*Drop everything. I love you. Come away with me now to Florida,*' you'd follow them. ¶"Yours is the blonde checkout clerk at Jensen's, isn't it? You've told me about as much. Dag's is probably Elvissa" (Elvissa is Claire's good friend) "—and *mine*, unfortunately," she comes out of the bathroom, head cocked to one side inserting an earring, "is Tobias. Life is *so* unfair, Andy. It really *is*." ¶Tobias is Claire's unfortunate obsession from New

York, and he's driving in from LAX airport this morning. He's our age, and Biff-and-Muffy private schoolish like Claire's brother Allan, and from some eastern white bread ghetto: New Rochelle? Shaker Heights? Darien? Westmount? Lake Forest? Does it matter? He has one of those bankish money jobs of the sort that when, at parties, he tells you what he does, you start to forget as soon as he tells you. He affects a tedious corporate killspeak. He sees nothing silly or offensive in frequenting franchised theme-restaurants with artificial, possessive-case names like McTuckey's or O'Dooligan's. He knows all variations and nuances of tassel loafers. ("I could *never* wear *your* shoes, Andy. They've got *moccasin* stitching. Far too casual.")

Not surprisingly, he's a control freak and considers himself informed. He likes to make jokes about paving Alaska and nuking Iran. To borrow a phrase from a popular song, he's loyal to the Bank of America. He's thrown something away and he's *mean*.

But then Tobias also has circus-freak-show good looks, so Dag and I are envious. Tobias could stand on a downtown corner at midnight and cause a traffic gridlock. It's too depressing for normal looking Joes. "He'll never have to work a day in his life if he doesn't want to," says Dag. "Life is not fair." Something about Tobias always extracts the phrase "life's not fair" from people.

ECONOMY
OF
SCALE
IS
RUINING
CHOICE

He and Claire met at Brandon's apartment in West Hollywood a few months ago. As a trio, they were all going to go to a Wall of Voodoo concert, but Tobias and Claire never made it, ending up instead at the Java coffee house, where Tobias talked and Claire stared for the night. Later on, Tobias kicked Brandon out of his own apartment. "Didn't hear a word Tobias said the entire evening," Claire says. "He could have been reading the menu backward for all I know. His profile, I tell you, it's *deadly*."

They spent that night together, and the next morning Tobias waltzed into the bedroom with one hundred long-stemmed roses, and he woke Claire up by gently lobbing them into her face, one by one. Then once she was fully awake, he heaped blood red Niagaras of stem and petal onto her body, and when Claire told Dag and me about this, even we had to concede that it was a wonderful gesture on his part.

"It had to be the most romantic moment of my life," said Claire. "I mean is it possible to die from roses? From plea-sure? Anyhow, later that morning we were in the car driving over to the farmers' market at Fairfax for brunch and to do the *L.A. Times* crossword puzzle with the pigeons and tourists in the outdoor area. Then on La Cienega Boulevard I saw this huge plywood sign with the words *100 Roses only $9.95* spray painted on it, and my heart just sank like a corpse wrapped in steel and tossed into the Hudson River. Tobias slunk down in his seat really low. Then things got *worse*. There was a red light and the guy from the booth comes over to the car and says something like, 'Mr. Tobias! My best customer! You're some lucky young lady to always be

---

Bread and Circuits: The electronic era tendency to view party politics as corny – no longer relevant or meaningful or useful to modern societal issues, and in many cases dangerous.

Voter's Block: The attempt, however futile, to register dissent with the current political system by simply not voting.

getting flowers from Mr. Tobias here!' As you can imagine, there was a pall over breakfast."

Okay okay. I'm being one-sided here. But it's fun to trash Tobias. It's easy. He embodies to me all of the people of my own generation who used all that was good in themselves just to make money; who use their votes for short-term gain. Who ended up blissful in the bottom-feeding jobs – marketing, land flipping, ambulance chasing, and money brokering. Such smugness. They saw themselves as eagles building mighty nests of oak branches and bullrushes, when instead they were really more like the eagles here in California, the ones who built their nests from tufts of abandoned auto parts looking like sprouts picked off a sandwich – rusted colonic mufflers and herniated fan belts – gnarls of freeway flotsam from the bleached grass meridians of the Santa Monica freeway: plastic lawn chairs, Styrofoam cooler lids, and broken skis – cheap, vulgar, toxic items that will either decompose in minutes or remain essentially unchanged until our galaxy goes supernova.

Oh, I don't hate Tobias. And as I hear his car pull into a stall outside, I realize that I see in him something that *I* might have become, something that all of us can become in the absence of vigilance. Something bland and smug that trades on its mask, filled with such rage and such contempt for humanity, such need, that the only food left for such a creature is their own flesh. He is like a passenger on a plane full of diseased people that crashes high in the mountains, and the survivors, not trusting each other's organs, snack on their own forearms.

"Candy, *baby!*" Tobias bellows mock heartily, slamming my screen door after finding Claire's place empty save for a heap of Dag. I wince, feigning interest in a *TV Guide* and mumbling

EROTICIZE

INTELLIGENCE

a hello. He sees the magazine: "Bottom feeding, are we? I thought you were the intellectual."

"Funny you should mention bottom feeding, Tobias—"

"What's that?" he barks, like someone with a Sony Walkman going full volume being asked for directions. Tobias doesn't pay any real attention to objects not basking entirely in his sphere.

"Nothing, Tobias. Claire's in the bathroom," I add, pointing in that direction the exact moment Claire rounds the corner chattering and putting a little girl's barrette in her hair.

"Tobias!" she says, running over for a little kiss, but Tobias is nonplussed by finding her so intimate in my environment and refuses a kiss.

"Excuse *me*," he says. "Looks like I'm interrupting something here." Claire and I roll our eyes at the whole notion that Tobias sees life as a not-very-funny French-restoration comedy aimed solely at him. Claire reaches up and kisses him anyway. (He's tall, of course.)

"Dag spilled plutonium all over my bungalow last night. He and Andy are going to clean it up today, and till then, I'm camped out here on the couch. Soon as Dag detoxes, that is. He's passed out on *my* couch. He was in New Mexico last week."

"I should have guessed he'd do something stupid like that. Was he building a bomb with it?"

"It wasn't plutonium," I add. "It was Trinitite, and it's harmless."

Armanism: After Giorgio Armani: an obsession with mimicking the seamless and (more importantly) *controlled* ethos of Italian couture. Like *Japanese Minimalism*, *Armanism* reflects a profound inner need for control.

Poor Buoyancy: The realization that one was a better person when one had less money.

Tobias ignores this. "What was he doing in your place, any-how?"

"Tobias, what am I, your *heifer*? He's my friend. Andy's my friend. I live here, remember?"

Tobias grabs her waist – looks like he's getting frisky. "Looks like I'm going to have to fillet you right down the middle, young lady." He yanks her crotch toward his, and I am just too embarrassed for words. Do people really talk like this? "Hey, Candy – looks like she's getting uppity. What do you say – should I impregnate her?"

At this point Claire's face indicates that she is well aware of feminist rhetoric and dialectic but is beyond being able to extract an appropriate quote. She actually *giggles*, realizing as she does so that that giggle will be used against her in some future, more lucid, less hormonal moment.

Tobias pulls Claire out the door. "I vote that we go to Dag's place for a while. Candy – tell your pal not to disturb us for a few hours should he decide to rise. Ciao."

The door slams once more, and, as with most couples im-patiently on their way to couple, there are no polite good-byes.

EAT
YOUR
PARENTS

We're hoovering plutonium out from the floorboards of Claire's living room. *Plutonium* – that's our new hipster code word for the rogue, possibly radioactive Trinitite beads. ¶"Feisty little buggers," blurts Dag as he thwacks a nozzle at a problematic wood knot, in good cheer and far more himself after twelve hours of sleep, a shower, a grapefruit from the MacArthurs' tree next door – a tree we helped string with blue Christmas lights last week – as well as the Dagmar Bellinghausen secret hangover cure (four Tylenol and a lukewarm tin of Campbell's Chicken & Stars soup). "These beads are like killer bees, the way they invade everything." ¶I spent the morning on the phone arranging and being preoccupied with my upcoming trip to Portland to see my family, a trip that Claire and Dag both say is making me morbid. "Cheer up. You have *nada* to worry about. Look at me. I just made someone's apartment uninhabitable for the next four and a half billion years. Imagine the guilt *I* must feel." ¶Dag's actually being generous about the plutonium matter, but he *did* have to make a psychic trade-off, and now he has to pretend he doesn't mind Claire and Tobias copulating in his bedroom, staining his sheets

(Tobias brags about not using condoms), dealphabetizing his cassette tapes, and looting his Kelvinator of citrus products. Nonetheless, the subject of Tobias is on Dag's mind: "I don't trust him. What's he up to?"

"Up to?"

"Andrew, wake up. Someone with his looks could have any bimbette with a toe separator in the state of California. That's obviously his style. But then he chooses Claire, who, *love* her as much as we do, *chic* as she may be, and *much* to her credit, is something of a flawed catch by Tobias standards. I mean, Andy, Claire *reads*. You *know* what I'm saying."

"I think so."

"He's not a nice human being, Andrew, and he even drove over the mountains to see her. And pllll-*eeze* don't try to tell me that somehow it's love."

"Maybe there's something about him we don't know, Dag. Maybe we should just have faith in him. Give him a reading list to help him better himself—"

A frosty stare.

"I think not, Andrew. He's too far gone. You can only minimize the damage with his type. Here – help me lift this table."

We rearrange the furniture, discovering new regions the plutonium has colonized. The rhythm of detoxification continues: brushes, rags, and dustpans. Sweep, sweep, sweep.

I ask if Dag is going to go visit his somewhat estranged parents in Toronto this Christmas. "Spare me, Andrew. *This* funster's having a cactus Christmas. Look," he says, changing the subject, "—*chase that dust bunny.*"

I change the subject. "I don't think my mother really grasps the concept of ecology or recycling," I start to tell Dag. "At Thanksgiving two years ago, after dinner, my mother was bagging all of the dinner trash into a huge nonbiodegradable bag. I pointed out to her that the bag was nonbiodegradable and she might want to consider using one of the degradable bags that were sitting on the shelf. She says to me, 'You're right! I forgot I had them!' and so she grabs one of the good bags. She then takes all of the trash, bad bag and all, and heaves it into the new one. The expression on her face was so genuinely proud that I didn't have the heart to tell her she'd gotten it all wrong. Louise Palmer: *Planet Saver*."

I flop down on the cool soft couch while Dag continues cleaning: "You should see my parents' place, Dag. It's like a museum of fifteen years ago. Nothing ever changes there; they're terrified of the future. Have you ever wanted to set your parents' house on fire just to get them out of their rut? Just so they had *some* change in their lives? At least Claire's parents get divorced every now and then. Keeps things lively. Home is like one of those aging European cities like Bonn or Antwerp or Vienna or Zürich, where there are no young people and it feels like an expensive waiting room."

"Andy, I'm the last person to be saying this, but, hey – your parents are only getting old. That's what happens to old people. They go cuckoo; they get boring, they lose their edge."

"These are *my* parents, Dag. I know them better than that." But Dag is all too right, and accuracy makes me feel embarrassingly petty. I parry his observation. I turn on him: "Fine comment coming from someone whose entire sense of life begins and ends in the year his own parents got married, as if that was the last year in which things could ever be safe. From someone who dresses like a General Motors showroom salesman from the year 1955. And, Dag, have you ever

noticed that your bungalow looks more like it belongs to a pair of Eisenhower era Allentown, Pennsylvania newlyweds than it does to a fin de siècle existentialist poseur?"

"Are you through yet?"

"No. You have Danish modern furniture; you use a black rotary-dial phone; you revere the Encyclopedia Britannica. You're just as afraid of the future as my parents."

Silence.

"Maybe you're right, Andy, and maybe you're upset about going home for Christmas—"

"Stop being nurturing. It's embarrassing."

"Very well. But *ne dump pas* on *moi*, okay? I've got my own demons and I'd prefer not to have them trivialized by your Psych 101-isms. We're always analyzing life too much. It's going to be the downfall of us all.

"I was going to suggest you take a lesson from my brother Matthew, the jingle writer. Whenever he phones or faxes his agent, they always haggle over who eats the fax – who's going to write it off as a business expense. And so I suggest you do the same thing with your parents. Eat them. Accept them as a part of getting you to here, and get on with life. Write them off as a business expense. At least your parents talk about Big Things. *I* try to talk about things like nuclear issues that matter to me with my parents and it's like I'm speaking Bratislavan. They listen indulgently to me for an appropriate length of time, and then after I'm out of wind, they ask me why I live in such a God-forsaken place like the Mojave Desert and how my love life is. Give parents the tiniest of

---

Musical Hairsplitting: The act of classifying music and musicians into pathologically picayune categories: *"The Vienna Franks are a good example of urban white acid folk revivalism crossed with ska."*

101-ism: The tendency to pick apart, often in minute detail, all aspects of life using half-understood pop psychology as a tool.

confidences and they'll use them as crowbars to jimmy you open and rearrange your life with no perspective. Sometimes I'd just like to mace them. I want to tell them that I envy their upbringings that were so clean, so free of *futurelessness*. And I want to throttle them for blithely handing over the world to us like so much skid-marked underwear."

PURCHASED
EXPERIENCES
DON'T COUNT

"Check *that* out," says Dag, a few hours later, pulling the car over to the side of the road and pointing to the local Institute for the Blind. "Notice anything funny?" ¶At first I see nothing untoward, but then it dawns on me that the Desert Moderne style building is landscaped with enormous piranha-spiked barrel cactuses, lovely but razor deadly; visions of plump little *Far Side* cartoon children bursting like breakfast sausages upon impact enter my head. ¶It's hot out. We're returning from Palm Desert, where we drove to rent a floor polisher, and on the way back we rattled past the Betty Ford Clinic (slowly) and then past the Eisenhower facility, where Mr. Liberace died. ¶"Hang on a second; I want to get a few of those spines for the charmed object collection." Dag pulls a pair of pliers and a Zip-Loc plastic bag from the clapped-out glove box which is held closed with a bungie cord. He then jackrabbits across the traffic hell of Ramon Road. ¶Two hours later the sun is high and the floor polisher lies exhausted on Claire's tiles. Dag, Tobias, and I are lizard lounging in the demilitarized zone of the kidney-shaped swimming pool central to our bungalows. Claire and her friend Elvissa are female bonding in my kitchen, drinking little cappuccinos and writing with chalks on my black wall. ¶A truce has been affected between the three of us guys out by the pool, and to his credit, Tobias has been rather amusing, telling tales of his recent trip to Europe – Eastern bloc toilet paper: "crinkly and shiny, like a K-Mart flyer in the *L.A. Times*," and "the pilgrimage" – visiting the grave of Jim Morrison at the Père Lachaise cemetery in Paris: "It was super easy to find. People had spray painted 'This way to Jimmy's' all over the tombstones of all these dead French poets. It was great."

Poor France.

Elvissa is Claire's good friend. They met months ago at Claire's doodad and bijou counter at I. Magnin. Unfortunately, Elvissa isn't her *real* name. Her real name is Catherine. *Elvissa* was my creation, a name that stuck from the very first time I ever used it (much to her pleasure) when Claire brought her home for lunch months ago. The name stems from her large, anatomically disproportionate head, like that of a woman who points to merchandise on a TV game show. This head is capped by an Elvis-oidal Mattel toy doll jet-black hairdo that frames her skull like a pair of inverted single quotes. And while she may not be *beautiful* per se, like most big-eyed women, she's compelling. Also, in spite of living in the desert, she's as pale as cream cheese and she's as thin as a greyhound chasing a pace bunny. Subsequently, she will seem a little bit cancer prone.

Although their background orbits are somewhat incongruous, Claire and Elvissa share a common denominator – both are headstrong, both have a healthy curiosity, but most important, both left their old lives behind them and set forth to make new lives for themselves in the name of adventure. In their similar quest to find a personal truth, they willingly put themselves on the margins of society, and this, I think, took some guts. It's harder for women to do this than men.

Conversation with Elvissa is like having a phone call with a noisy child from the deep South – Tallahassee, Florida, to be exact – but a child speaking from a phone located in Sydney, Australia, or Vladivostok in the USSR. There's a satellite time lag between replies, maybe one-tenth of a second long, that makes you think there's something suspect malfunctioning in your brain – information and secrets being withheld from you.

As for how Elvissa makes her living, none of us is quite sure, and none of us is sure we want to even *know*. She is living proof of Claire's theory that anyone who lives in a resort town under the age of thirty is on the make. I *think* her work may have to do with pyramid or Ponzi schemes, but then it may be somehow sexual: I once saw her in a Princess Stephanie one-piece swimsuit ("please, my *maillot*") chatting amiably with a mafioso type while counting a wad of bills at the poolside of the Ritz Carlton, high in the graham cracker-colored hills above Rancho Mirage. Afterward she denied she was there. *When pressed*, she will admit to selling never-to-be-seen vitamin shampoos, aloe products, and Tupperware containers, on which subject she is able to improvise convincing antiweevil testimonials on the spot ("This crisper saved my *life*").

Elvissa and Claire exit my bungalow. Claire appears both

depressed and preoccupied, eyes focused on an invisible object hovering above the ground a body's length in front of her. Elvissa, however, is in a pleasant state and is wearing an ill-fitting 1930s swimsuit, which is her attempt to be hip and retro. In Elvissa's mind this afternoon is her "time to be Young and do Young things with Young people my own age." She thinks of us as Youngsters. But her choice of swimwear merely accentuates how far removed she has become from current bourgeois time/space. Some people don't have to play the hip game; I like Elvissa, but she can be so clued out.

"Check out the Vegas housewife on chemotherapy," whispers Tobias to me and Dag, misguidedly trying to win our confidence through dumb wisecracks.

"We love you, too, Tobias," replies Dag, after which he smiles up at the girls and says, "Hi, kids. Have a nice chat?" Claire listlessly grunts and Elvissa smiles. Dag hops up to kiss Elvissa while Claire flops out on a sun-bleached yellow fold-out deck chair. The overall effect around the pool is markedly 1949, save for Tobias's Day-Glo green swimsuit.

"Hi, Andy," Elvissa whispers, bending down to peck me on the cheek. She then mumbles a cursory hello to Tobias, after which she grabs her own lounger to begin the arduous task of covering every pore of her body with PABA 29, her every move under the worshipful looks of Dag, who is like a

BENCH
PRESS
YOUR
I.Q.

friendly dog unfortunately owned by a never-at-home master. Claire's body on the other side of Dag is totally rag-doll slack with gloom. Did she receive bad news, or something?

"Pretty day today, isn't it?" Elvissa says to no one in particular.

"Well *this* lab rat here just can't stop pushing the lever to release the pleasure pellets."

"You're weirding me out already, Dag," she replies. "Please stop."

A silent, animal hour passes. Tobias, no longer the center of attention with his Eurobragging, starts to thrash. He sits up, does a minor preen, inspects the bulge in his shorts, and cat-paws his hair. "Well, Dagwood" (he says to Dag*mar*) "looks like you've been hitting the weights since the last time I saw you out in public stopping traffic with your bod."

Dag and I, both on our stomachs, look at each other, grimace, then tell Tobias in stereo to "get a life." This forces him to shift his focus onto Claire, whose face is snarfed into the recline-o-lounger and not good for anything. Ever noticed how impossible it is to rile a depressed person.

He then shifts his predatory eyes on Elvissa, now doing her nails in Honolulu Choo-Choo pink nail polish. His is a look that obviously feels superior to the receiver of his gaze. I can just *see* him wearing this same expression while he wears a blue Savile Row suit, indulging in nutritional slumming in a New York cafeteria at lunch hour – every waitress a conquest and proof of his *droit de seigneur*.

"What are *you* looking at, yuppie boy?"

"I am *not* a yuppie."

"Like hell you're not."

"I'm too young. I don't have enough money. I may *look* the part, but it's *only* looks. By the time goodies like cheap land and hot jobs got to me they just sort of . . . *started running out*."

A sensation! Tobias not rich enough? This admission tweaks me out of my own thoughts – the way breaking a shoelace when tying a shoe can somehow instantaneously shift you into a new plane of consciousness. I realize that Tobias, in spite of his mask, is *shin jin rui* – X generation – just like us.

He *also* knows that he's the center of attention again: "To be honest, trying to look like a yuppie is pretty exhausting. I think I might even give up the whole ruse – there's no payoff. I might *even* become a bohemian like *these three*. Maybe move into a cardboard box on top of the RCA building; stop eating protein; work as live bait at Gator World. Why, I might *even move out here to the desert*."

(Perish the thought.)

"Spare me, *please*," retaliates Elvissa. "I know your type exactly. You yuppies are all the same and I am fed up indeed with the likes of you. Let me see your eyes."

"What?"

"*Let me see your eyes*."

Tobias leans over to allow Elvissa to put a hand around his jaw and extract information from his eyes, the blue color of Dutch souvenir plates. She takes an awfully long time. "Well, okay. Maybe you're not all *that* bad. I *might* even tell you a special story in a few minutes. Remind me. But it depends. I want you to tell me something first: after you're dead and buried and floating around whatever place we go to, what's going to be your best memory of Earth?"

"What do you mean? I don't get it."

"What one moment for you defines what it's like to be alive on this planet. What's your *takeaway*?"

There is a silence. Tobias doesn't get her point, and frankly, neither do I. She continues: "Fake yuppie experiences that you had to spend money on, like white water rafting or elephant

---

Yuppie Wannabes: An X generation subgroup that believes the myth of a yuppie life-style being both satisfying and viable. Tend to be highly in debt, involved in some form of substance abuse, and show a willingness to talk about Armageddon after three drinks.

rides in Thailand don't count. I want to hear some small moment from your life that *proves you're really alive*."

Tobias does not readily volunteer any info. I think he needs an example first.

"I've got one," says Claire.

All eyes turn to her.

"Snow," she says to us. "Snow."

REMEMBER
EARTH
CLEARLY

"Snow," says Claire, at the very moment a hailstorm of doves erupts upward from the brown silk soil of the MacArthurs' yard next door. ¶The MacArthurs have been trying to seed their new lawn all week, but the doves just love those tasty little grass seeds. And doves being so cute and all, it's impossible to be genuinely angry with them. Mrs. MacArthur (Irene) halfheartedly shoos them away every so often, but the doves simply fly up on top of the roof of their house, where they consider themselves hidden, at which point they throw exciting little dove parties. ¶"I'll always remember the first time I saw snow. I was twelve and it was just after the first and biggest divorce. I was in New York visiting my mother and was standing beside a traffic island in the middle of Park Avenue. I'd never been out of L.A. before. I was entranced by the big city. I was looking up at the Pan Am Building and contemplating the essential problem of Manhattan." ¶"Which is —?" I ask. ¶"Which is that there's too much weight improperly distributed: towers and elevators; steel, stone, and cement. So much *mass* up so high that gravity itself could end up being warped — some dreadful inversion – an exchange program with the sky."

(I love it when Claire gets weird.) "I was shuddering at the thought of this. But *right then* my brother Allan yanked at my sleeve because the walk signal light was green. And when I turned my head to walk across, my face went *bang*, right into my first snowflake ever. It melted in my eye. I didn't even know what it *was* at first, but then I saw *millions* of flakes – all white and smelling like ozone, floating downward like the shed skins of angels. Even Allan stopped. Traffic was honking at us, but time stood still. And so, *yes* – if I take *one* memory of earth away with me, that moment will be the one. To this day I consider my right eye charmed."

"Perfect," says Elvissa. She turns to Tobias. "Get the drift?"

"Let me think a second."

"I've got one," says Dag with some enthusiasm, partially the result, I suspect, of his wanting to score brownie points with Elvissa. "It happened in 1974. In Kingston, Ontario." He lights a cigarette and we wait. "My dad and I were at a gas station and I was given the task of filling up the gas tank – a Galaxy 500, snazzy car. And filling it up was a big responsibility for me. I was one of those goofy kids who always got colds and never got the hang of things like filling up gas tanks or unraveling tangled fishing rods. I'd always screw things up somehow; break something; have it die.

"Anyway, Dad was in the station shop buying a map, and I was outside feeling so manly and just *so* proud of how I hadn't botched anything up yet – set fire to the gas station or what have you – and the tank was *al*most full. Well, Dad came out just as I was topping the tank off, at which point the nozzle simply went nuts. It started spraying all over. I don't know why – it just *did* – all over my jeans, my running shoes, the license plate, the cement – like purple alcohol. Dad saw everything and I thought I was going to catch total shit. I felt so small. But instead he smiled and said to me, 'Hey, Sport. Isn't the smell of gasoline great? Close your eyes and inhale. So *clean*. It smells like the *future*.'

"Well, I did that – I closed my eyes just as he asked, and breathed in deeply. And at that point I saw the bright orange light of the sun coming through my eyelids, smelled the gasoline and my knees buckled. But it was the most perfect moment of my life, and so if you ask me (and I have a lot of my hopes pinned on this), heaven just *has* to be an awful lot like those few seconds. That's my memory of Earth."

"Was it leaded or unleaded?" asks Tobias.

"Leaded," replies Dag.

"Perfect."

"Andy?" Elvissa looks to me. "You?"

"I know my Earth memory. It's a smell – the smell of bacon. It was a Sunday morning at home and we were all having breakfast, an unprecedented occurrence since me and all six of my brothers and sisters inherited my mother's tendency to detest the sight of food in the morning. We'd sleep in instead.

"Anyhow, there wasn't even a special reason for the meal. All nine of us simply ended up in the kitchen by accident, with everyone being funny and nice to each other, and reading out the grisly bits from the newspaper. It was sunny; no one was being psycho or mean.

"I remember very clearly standing by the stove and frying a batch of bacon. I knew even then that this was the only such morning our family would ever be given – a morning where we would all be normal and kind to each other and know that we liked each other without any strings attached – and that soon enough (and we did) we would all become batty and distant the way families invariably do as they get along in years.

"And so I was close to tears, listening to everyone make jokes and feeding the dog bits of egg; I was feeling homesick for the event while it was happening. All the while my forearms were getting splattered by little pinpricks of hot bacon grease, but I wouldn't yell. To me, those pinpricks were no more and no less pleasurable than the pinches my sisters used to give me to extract from me the truth about which one I loved the most – and it's those little pinpricks and the smell of bacon that I'm going to be taking away with me; that will be my memory of Earth."

Tobias can barely contain himself. His body is poised forward, like a child in a shopping cart waiting to lunge for the presweetened breakfast cereals: "I know what my memory is! I know what it is now!"

"Well just *tell* us, then," says Elvissa.

"It's like this –" (God only knows what *it* will be) "Every summer back in Tacoma Park" (Washington, D.C. I *knew* it was an eastern city) "my dad and I would rig up a shortwave radio that he had left over from the 1950s. We'd string a wire across the yard at sunset and tether it up to the linden tree to act as an antenna. We'd try all of the bands, and if the radiation in the Van Allen belt was low, then we'd pick up just about everywhere: Johannesburg, Radio Moscow, Japan, Punjabi stuff. But more than anything we'd get signals from South America, these weird haunted-sounding bolero-samba music transmissions from dinner theaters in Ecuador and Caracas and Rio. The music would come in faintly – faintly but clearly.

"One night Mom came out onto the patio in a pink sundress and carrying a glass pitcher of lemonade. Dad swept her into his arms and they danced to the samba music with Mom still holding the pitcher. She was squealing but loving it. I think she was enjoying that little bit of danger the threat of broken glass added to the dancing. And there were crickets cricking and the transformer humming on the power lines behind the garages, and I had my suddenly young parents all to myself – them and this faint music that sounded like heaven – faraway, clear, and impossible to contact – coming from this faceless place where it was always summer and where beautiful people were always dancing and where it was impossible to call by telephone, even if you wanted to. Now *that's* Earth to me."

Ultra Short Term Nostalgia: Homesickness for the extremely recent past: *"God, things seemed so much better in the world last week."*

Well, who'd have thought Tobias was capable of such thoughts? We're going to have to do a reevaluation of the lad.

"Now you have to tell me the story you promised," says Tobias to Elvissa, who seems saddened by the prospect, as though she has to keep a bet she regrets having made.

"Of course. Of course I will," she says. "Claire tells me you people tell stories sometimes, so you won't find it too stupid. You're *none* of you allowed to make any cracks, okay?"

"Hey," I say, "that's always been our main rule."

CHANGE COLOUR

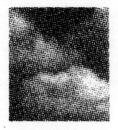

Elvissa starts her tale: "It's a story I call 'The Boy with the Hummingbird Eyes.' So if all of you will please lean back and relax now, I will tell it. ¶"It starts in Tallahassee, Florida, where I grew up. There was this boy next door, Curtis, who was best friends with my brother Matt. My mother called him Lazy Curtis because he just drawled his way through life, rarely speaking, silently chewing bologna sandwiches inside his lantern jaw and hitting baseballs farther than anyone else whenever he got up the will to do so. He was just *so* wonderfully silent. So *competent* at everything. I, of course, madly adored Curtis ever from the first moment our U-haul pulled up to the new house and I saw him lying on the grass next door smoking a cigarette, an act that made my mother just about faint. He was maybe only fifteen. ¶"I promptly copied everything about him. Most superficially I copied his hair (which I still indirectly feel is slightly his to this day), his sloppy T-shirts and his lack of speech and his panthery walk. So did my brother. And the three of us shared what are still to me the best times of our lives walking around the subdivision we lived in, a development that somehow never got fully built.

We'd play war inside these tract houses that had been reclaimed by palm trees and mangroves and small animals that had started to make their homes there, too: timid armadillos in pink bathtubs lying on a bed of leaves; sparrows flying in and out of front doors that opened to nothing but a hot white Gulf sky; windows shaded by smoky Spanish moss. Mom, of course, was petrified about alligators, but Lazy Curtis said he'd wrestle one if it tried to attack me. So of course I couldn't *wait* for one to come by.

"In our war games I was always Nurse Meyers and had to patch up Curtis's wounds, wounds which, as time passed, became suspiciously groin centered, needing 'cures' that became increasingly elaborate. A decaying master bedroom deep within the Forgotten Subdivision was our mobile hospital. Matt was sent home to fetch rations, Rice Krispie Squares and Space Food Stix. In the interim I would have to perform ritualistic groin cures of Curtis's invention with names influenced by his tabloidal reading tastes: the 'Tripoli Hershey Bar Massage' and the 'Hanoi Canteen Slut Mud Rub.' About the only thing Curtis read was *Soldier of Fortune*, the names of these procedures meant nothing to me, except for years later when, in retrospect, they made me giggle.

"I lost my virginity with Curtis there in that dreamy, swampy room, but it was with such great affection that even *now* I think I was luckier than most women I've met and whose defloration stories I've heard. I was so utterly dreadfully attached to Curtis, like only a teen bride can be. And so when his family moved away when I was fifteen, I didn't eat for two weeks. And, of *course*, he never so much as wrote me a postcard – I didn't expect him to, it wasn't his style. I was so lost for so *long* without him. But life went on.

"It was maybe fourteen years before Curtis reached the status of painless memory, and I'd only think of him rarely – the smell of a stranger's similar sweat in an elevator or when I saw men of similar muscular aspect, more often than not guys like those ones who stand near freeway exits with felt-pen-on-cardboard signs saying Will Work for Food.

"Then a funny thing happened here in Palm Springs a few months ago—

"I was at the Spa de Luxembourg. I was waiting to give a demonstration of some aloe products to a hotel guest and had time to kill; I was lying poolside, enjoying the sun, which is something people who live in nice climates rarely do. In front of me there was a man seated in a fold-up chair, but because I entered the pool deck from the opposite direction, I didn't pay him any attention, save for noticing that he had a well-cut head of black hair and a hot bod. He would also occasionally bob his head up and down, then sideways, not like a spastic, but more as though he kept noticing something sexy from the corner of his eyes but was continually mistaken.

"Anyhow, this rich broad, this real *Sylvia* type" (Elvissa calls rich women with good haircuts and good clothes *Sylvias*) "comes out from the spa building going mince mince mince with her little shoey-wooeys and her Lagerfeld dress, right up to this guy in front of me. She purrrrs something I miss and then puts a little gold bracelet around this guy's wrist which he offers up to her (body language) with about as much enthusiasm as though he were waiting for her to vaccinate it. She gives the hand a kiss, says 'Be ready for nine o'clock' and then toddles off.

"So I'm curious.

"Very coolly I stroll over to the pool bar – the one you used to work in, Andy – and order a most genteel cocktail of the color pink, then saunter back to my perch, surreptitiously checking out the guy on the way back. But I think I died on the spot when I saw who it was. It was Curtis, of course.

"He was taller than I remembered, and he'd lost any baby fat he might have had, and his body had taken on a sinewy, pugilistic look, like those kids who shop for needle bleach on Hollywood Boulevard who sort of resemble German tourists from a block away and then you see them up close. Anyhow, there were a lot of ropey white scars all over him. And Lord! The boy had been to the tattoo parlor a few times. A crucifix blared from his inner left thigh and a locomotive engine roared across his left shoulder. Underneath the engine there was a heart with china-dish break marks; a bouquet of dice and gardenias graced the other shoulder. He'd obviously been around the block a few times.

"I said, 'Hello, Curtis,' and he looked up and said, 'Well I'll be damned! It's Catherine Lee Meyers!' I couldn't think of what to say next. I put down my drink and sat closed legged and slightly fetal on a chair beside him and stared and felt warm. He reached up and kissed me on the cheek and said, 'I missed you, Baby Doll. Thought I'd be dead before I ever saw you again.'

"The next few minutes were a blur of happiness. But before long I had to go. My client was calling. Curtis told me what he was doing in town, but I couldn't make out details – something about an acting job in L.A. (uh oh). But even while we were talking, he kept bobbing his head around to and fro looking at I don't know what. I asked him what he was looking at, and all he said was 'hummingbirds. Maybe I'll tell you more tonight.' He gave me his address (an apartment address, not a hotel), and we agreed to meet for dinner that night at eight thirty. I couldn't really say to him, '*But what about Sylvia?*' really *could I*, knowing that she had a nine o'clock appointment. I didn't want to seem snoopy.

"Anyhow, eight thirty rolled around, plus a little bit more. It was the night of that storm – remember that? I just *barely* made it over to the address, an ugly condo development from the 1970s, out near Racquet Club Drive in the windy part of town. The power was out so the streetlights were crapped out, too. The flash-flood wells in the streets were beginning to overflow and I tripped coming up the stairs of the apartment complex because there were no lights. The apartment, number three-something, was on the third floor, so I had to walk up this pitch-black stairwell to get there, only to be ignored when I knocked on the door. I was furious. As I was leaving, I yelled '*You have gone to the dogs, Curtis Donnely*,' at which point, hearing my voice, he opened the door.

"He'd been drinking. He said to not mind the apartment,

which belonged to a model friend of his named Lenni. 'Spelled with an *i*,' he said, 'you know how models are.'

This was obviously not the same little boy from Tallahassee.

"The apartment had no furniture, and owing to the power failure, no light, save for birthday candles, several boxes of which he had scavenged out of Lenni's kitchen drawer. Curtis was lighting them one by one. It was so dim.

I could faintly see that the walls were papered in a jetsam of black-and-white fashion photos ripped (not very *carefully* ripped, I might add) from fashion magazines. The room smelled like perfume sample strips. The models were predominantly male and pouting, with alien eyes and GQ statue bones that *mouéed* at us from all corners of the room. I tried to pretend I didn't notice them. After the age of twenty-five, Scotch taping magazine stuff to your walls is just plain scary.

"'Seems like we're destined to always end up meeting in primitive rooms, eh, Curtis?' I said, but I don't think he got the reference to our old mobile love hospital. We sat down on the floor on blankets near the sliding door and watched the storm outside. I had a quick Scotch to grab a buzz, but didn't want it to go past that. I wanted to remember the night.

"Anyhow, we had the slow, stunted conversation of people catching up with time. Every so often, as there is with strained reminiscences, there were occasional wan smiles, but mostly the mood was dry. I think we were both wondering if we'd made a mistake. He was maudlin drunk. Maybe he was going to cry soon.

"Then there was a banging on the door. It was Sylvia.

"'Oh fuck, it's Kate,' he whispered. 'Don't say anything. Make her wear herself out. Make her go away.'

"Kate was a force of nature outside the door in the black black hallway. Certainly not the meek little Sylvia of that afternoon. She'd make the devil blush with the names she was calling Curtis, demanding that he let her in, accusing him of banging and getting banged by anything that breathes and has a wallet, then quickly refining that to anything with a *wallet*. She was demanding her 'charms' back and threatening to have one of her husband's goons go after his 'one remaining orchid.' The neighbors, if not horrified, must at least have been fascinated.

"But Curtis just held me tight and said zero. Kate eventually spent herself out, whimpered, then soundlessly vacated the premises. Soon we heard a car roar and tires squeal down in the building's parkade.

"I was uncomfortable, but unlike the neighbors, *I* could sate my curiosity. Before I could ask a question, though, Curtis said 'Don't ask. Ask me about something else. *Anything* else. But not *that*.'

"'Very well,' I said. 'Let's talk about hummingbirds,' which made him laugh and roll over. I was glad at least that some of the tension was gone. He then started taking off his pants, saying, 'Don't worry. You don't *want* to make it with me anyway. Trust me on *that* one, Baby Doll.' Then, once he was naked, he opened his legs and cupped his hands to his crotch, saying 'Look.' Sure enough, there was just one 'orchid.'

"'That happened down in—' he said, me stupidly forgetting the name of the country, someplace Central America, I think. He called it 'the servants' quarters.'

"He laid back on the blanket, Scotch bottle at his side and told me about his fighting for pay in wars down there. Of discipline and camaraderie. Of secret paychecks from men with Italian accents. Finally, he was relaxing.

"He went on at some length about his exploits, most of them about as interesting to me as watching ice hockey on TV,

but I kept up a good show of interest. But then he started mentioning one name more than others, the name *Arlo*. Arlo, I take it, was his best friend, something more than that – whatever it is that men become during a war, and who knows what else.

"Anyhow, one day Curtis and Arlo were out 'on a shoot,' when the fighting got life-threateningly intense. They were forced to lie down on the ground, covered in camouflage, with their primed machine guns pointed at the enemy. Arlo was lying next to Curtis and they were both hair-trigger itching to shoot. Suddenly, this hummingbird started darting into Arlo's eyes. Arlo brushed it away, but it kept darting back. Then there were two and then *three* hummingbirds. 'What the hell are they doing?' asked Curtis, and Arlo explained that some hummingbirds are attracted to the color blue and that they dart at it in an attempt to collect it to build their nests, and what they were trying to do was build their nests with Arlo's eyes.

"At that point Curtis said, 'Hey, my eyes are blue, too—' but Arlo's sweeping gestures to move the birds out of his eyes attracted the enemy fire. They were attacked. That was when a bullet entered Curtis's groin and when another bullet entered Arlo's heart, killing him instantly.

"What happened next, I don't know. But the next day Curtis joined the mop-up crews, in spite of his injury, and returned to the battle site to collect and bag the dead bodies. But when they found the body of *Arlo*, they were all as aghast as anybody who picks up bodies regularly can be, not because of his bullet wounds, (a common enough sight) but because of a horrible sacrilege that had been performed on his corpse – the blue meat of Arlo's eyes had been picked away from the whites. The native men cursed and crossed themselves, but Curtis merely closed Arlo's eyelids then kissed each one. He knew about the hummingbirds; he kept that knowledge to himself.

"He was 4-F'ed that day, and by nightfall was numb and on a plane back to the States, where he ended up in San Diego.

And at that point his life becomes a blank. That's when all of the things he wouldn't tell me started to happen.

"'So *that's* why you're looking at the hummingbirds all the time, then,' I said. But there was more. Lying there on the floor, lit by a sad triad of three birthday candles that also illuminated a sullen beefcake on the bedroom wall, he began to cry. Oh, God, *weep* is the right word. He wasn't crying. He was weeping and I could only place my chin on his heart and listen – listen while he blubbered that he didn't know what happened to his youth, to any of his ideas about people or niceness, and that he had become a slightly freaky robot. 'I can't even break into *porno* now because of my accident. Not and get top dollar.'

"And after a while we just laid there and breathed together. He started to talk to me, but his talk was like a roulette wheel that's almost slowed down to a full stop. 'You *know*, Baby Doll,' he said, 'sometimes you can be very stupid and swim a bit too far out into the ocean and not have enough energy to swim back to shore. Birds insult you at that point, when you're out there just *floating*. They only remind you of the land you'll never be able to reach again. But *one* of these days, I don't know *when*, one of those little hummingbirds is going to zip right in and make a dart for *my* blue little eyes, and when that happens—'

"But he never told me what he was going to do. It wasn't his intention; he passed out instead. It must have been midnight by then and I was left staring at his poor, battle-scarred body, under the birthday candle lighting. I tried to think of something, *any*thing, I could do for him, and I only came up with one idea. I put my chest on top of his, and kissed him on the forehead, grabbing onto his tattoos of trains and dice and gardenias and broken hearts for support. And I tried to empty the contents of my soul into his. I imagined my strength – my soul – was a white laser beam shooting from my heart into his, like those light pulses in glass wires that can pump a million books to the moon in one second. This beam was cutting through his chest like a beam cutting through a sheet of steel.

Curtis could take or leave this strength that he so obviously lacked – but I just wanted it to be there for him as a reserve. I would give my *life* for that man, and all I was able to donate that night was whatever remained of my youth. No regrets.

"Anyway, sometime that night, after the rains ended and while I was sleeping, Curtis disappeared from the room. And unless fate throws us together again, which I doubt quite strongly, I suspect that was it for us for this lifetime. He's out there right now, maybe even as we speak, getting pecked in the eyeball by a ruby-throated little gem. And you know what'll happen to him when he *does* get pecked? Call it a hunch, but when that happens, train cars will shunt in his mind. And the next time *Sylvia* comes knocking on his door, he'll walk over and he'll *open* it. Call it a hunch."

None of us can talk, and it's obvious to us what Elvissa will remember Earth by. Fortunately, the phone rings in my bungalow and definitively cuts the moment, as only a phone ring can. Tobias takes that moment to excuse himself and head over to his car, and when I enter my bungalow to pick up the phone, I see him stooped down and looking at his eyes in his rented Nissan's rearview mirror. Right then I know that it's all over between him and Claire. Call it a hunch. I pick up the phone.

WHY
AM I
POOR?

It's Prince Tyler of Portland on the phone, my baby brother by some five years; our family's autumn crocus; the buzz-cut love child; spoiled little monster who hands a microwaved dish of macaroni back to Mom and commands, "There's a patch in the middle that's still cold. Reheat it." (Me, my two other brothers, or my three sisters would be *thwocked* on the head for such insolence, but such baronial dictums from *Tyler* merely reinforce his princely powers.) ¶"Hi, Andy. Bagging some rays?" ¶"Hi, Tyler. Actually I *am*." ¶"Too cool, too cool. Listen: Bill-cubed, the World Trade Center, Lori, Joanna, and me are coming down to stay in your spare bungalow on January 8 for five days. That's Elvis's birthday. We're going to have a KingFest. Any problem with that?" ¶"Not that I can think of, but you'll be packed like hamsters in there. Hope you don't mind. Let me check." (Bill-cubed, actually Bill³, is three of Tyler's friends, all named Bill; the World Trade Center is the Morrissey twins, each standing six feet six inches.) ¶I rummage through my bungalow, hunting for my reservations book (the landlord places me in charge of rentals). I muse all the while about Tyler and his clique – Global Teens, as he labels them, though most are in their twenties. It seems amusing and confusing – unnatural – to me the way Global Teens, or Tyler's friends, at least, live their lives so *together* with each other: shopping, traveling, squabbling, thinking, and breathing, just like the Baxter family. (Tyler, not surprisingly, has ended up becoming fast friends, via me, with Claire's brother Allan.)

How cliquish *are* these Global Teens? It really boggles. Not *one* of them can go to Waikiki for a simple one-week holiday, for example, without several enormous gift-laden send-off parties in one of three classic sophomoric themes: Tacky Tourist, Favorite Dead Celebrity, or Toga. And once they arrive there, nostalgic phone calls soon start: sentimental and complicated volleys of elaborately structured trans-Pacific conference calls flówing every other day, as though the jolly vacationer had just hurtled toward Jupiter on a three-year mission rather than six days of overpriced Mai Tais on Kuhio Street.

"The Tyler Set" can be really sucky, too – no drugs, no irony, and only moderate booze, popcorn, cocoa, and videos on Friday nights. And elaborate wardrobes – *such wardrobes!* Stunning and costly, coordinated with subtle sophistication, composed of only the finest labels. Slick. And they can afford them because, like most Global Teen princes and princesses, they all live at home, unable to afford what few ludicrously overpriced apartments exist in the city. So their money all goes on their backs.

Tyler is like that old character from TV, Danny Partridge, who didn't want to work as a grocery store box boy but instead wanted to start out owning the whole store. Tyler's

---

Rebellion Postponement: The tendency in one's youth to avoid traditionally youthful activities and artistic experiences in order to obtain serious career experience. Sometimes results in the mourning for lost youth at about age thirty, followed by silly haircuts and expensive joke-inducing wardrobes.

friends have nebulous, unsalable but *fun* talents – like being able to make really great coffee or owning a really *good* head of hair (oh, to see Tyler's shampoo, gel, and mousse collection!).

They're nice kids. None of their folks can complain. They're *perky*. They embrace and believe the pseudo-globalism and ersatz racial harmony of ad campaigns engineered by the makers of soft drinks and computer-inventoried sweaters. Many want to work for IBM when their lives end at the age of twenty-five (*"Excuse me, but can you tell me more about your pension plan?"*). But in some dark and undefinable way, these kids are also Dow, Union Carbide, General Dynamics, and the military. And I suspect that unlike Tobias, were their AirBus to crash on a frosty Andean plateau, they would have little, if any, compunction about eating dead fellow passengers. Only a theory.

Anyhow, a peek out my window while looking for the reservation book reveals that the poolside is now devoid of people. The door knocks and Elvissa quickly pops her head inside, "Just wanted to say bye, Andy."

"Elvissa – my brother's on hold long distance. Can you wait a sec?"

"No. This is best." She kisses me on the ridge at the top of my nose, between my eyes. A damp kiss that reminds me that girls like Elvissa, spontaneous, a tetch trashy but undoubtedly alive, are somehow never going to be intimate with constipated deadpan fellows like me. "Ciao, bambino," she says. "It's Splittsville for *this* little Neapolitan waif."

Conspicuous Minimalism: A life-style tactic similar to *Status Substitution*. The nonownership of material goods flaunted as a token of moral and intellectual superiority.

Café Minimalism: To espouse a philosophy of minimalism without actually putting into practice any of its tenets.

"You coming back soon?" I yell, but she's gone, off around the rose bushes and into, I see, Tobias's car.

Well, well, well.

Back on the phone: "Hi, Tyler. The eighth is fine."

"Good. We'll discuss the details at Christmas. You *are* coming up, aren't you?"

"Unfortunately, *oui*."

"I think it's going to be mondo weirdo this year, Andy. You'd better have an escape hatch ready. Book five different flight dates for leaving. Oh, and by the way, what do you *want* for Christmas?"

"Nothing, Tyler. I'm getting rid of all the things in my life."

"I worry about you, Andy. You have no ambition." I can hear him spooning yogurt. Tyler wants to work for a huge corporation. The bigger the better.

"There's nothing strange about not wanting anything, Tyler."

"So be it, then. Just make sure that *I* get all the loot you give away. And make sure it's *Polo*."

"Actually I was thinking of giving you a minimalist gift this year, Tyler."

"Huh?"

"Something like a nice rock or a cactus skeleton."

He pauses on the other end. "Are you on drugs?"

"No, Tyler. I thought an object of simple beauty might be appropriate. You're old enough now."

"You're laffaminit, Andy. A real screamfest. A rep tie and socks will do *perfectly*."

O'Propriation: The inclusion of advertising, packaging, and entertainment jargon from earlier eras in everyday speech for ironic and/or comic effect: *"Kathleen's Favorite Dead Celebrity party was tons o' fun"* or *"Dave really thinks of himself as a zany, nutty, wacky, and madcap guy, doesn't he?"*

My doorbell rings, then Dag walks in. Why does no one ever wait for me to answer the door? "Tyler, that's the doorbell. I have to go. I'll see you next week, okay?"

"Shoe eleven, waist thirty, Neck 15 and a half."

"Adios."

CELEBRITIES
DIE

It's three hours or so after Tyler's phone call, and people are weirding me out today. I just can't deal with it. Thank God I'm working tonight. Creepy as it may be, dreary as it may be, repetitive as it may be, work keeps me level. ¶Tobias gave Elvissa a ride home but never returned. Claire pooh-poohs the notion of hanky-panky. She seems to know something that I don't. Maybe she'll spill her secret later on. ¶Both Dag and Claire are sulking on the couches, not talking to each other. They're restlessly shelling peanuts, tossing the burlappy remnants into an overflowing 1974 Spokane World's Fair ashtray. (That was the fair where it rained a lot and where they had buildings made out of aluminum soda can tabs.) ¶Dag is upset that Elvissa gave him not one shred of attention today and Claire, because of the plutonium, still won't return into her house. The contamination business has bothered her more than we'd suspected. She claims she'll be living with me indefinitely now: "Radiation has more endurance than even Mr. Frank Sinatra, Andy. I'm here for the long haul." ¶Claire *will*, however, make forays into her residence – no longer than five minutes per foray per day – to retrieve her belongings. Her first trip was as timid a one as might be made by a medieval peasant entering a dying plague town, brandishing a dead goat to ward away evil spirits.

"How brave," snipes Dag, to which Claire shoots back an angry glare. I tell her I think she's overreacting. "Your place is *spotless*, Claire. You're acting like a techno-peasant."

"Both of you may laugh, but neither of you has a Chernobyl in their living room."

"True."

She spits out a mutant baby peanut and inhales. "Tobias is gone for good. I can tell. Imagine that, the best-looking human flesh I'll ever be in contact with – the Walking Orgasm – gone forever."

"I wouldn't say that, Claire," I say, even though in my heart I know she's right. "Maybe he just stopped for something to eat."

"Spare me, Andy. It's been three hours now. And he took his bag. I just *can't* figure out why he'd leave so suddenly."

I can.

The two dogs, meanwhile, stare hungrily at the nuts Dag and Claire are shelling.

"Know what the fastest way to get rid of dogs that beg at the dinner table is?" I ask, to a mumbled response. "Give them a piece of carrot or an olive instead of meat, and give it to them with an earnest face. They'll look at you like you're mad and they'll be gone in seconds. Granted, they might think *less of you*, too."

Claire has been ignoring me. "Of course, this means I'll have to follow him to New York." She stands up and heads to the door. "Looks like a white Christmas for me this year, boys. *God*, obsessions are awful." She looks at her face in the mirror hanging by the door. "Not even thirty and already my upper lip is beginning to shrink. I'm doomed." She leaves.

"I've dated three women in my life," says my boss and next-door neighbor, Mr. MacArthur, "and I married two of them."

It's later on at night at Larry's. Two real estate weenies from Indio are singing "wimmaway" into the open mike that belongs to our chanteuse Lorraine, currently taking a break from show-tuning along with her wheezy electronic "rhythm pal," and drinking white wine while oozing sad glamour at bar's end. It's a slow night; bad tips. Dag and I are drying glasses, a strangely restful activity, and we're listening to Mr. M. do his Mr. M. shtick. We feed him lines; it's like watching a Bob Hope TV special but with home viewer participation. He's never funny, but he's *funny*.

The evening's highlight was an elderly failed Zsa Zsa who vomited a storm of Sidecars onto the carpet beside the trivia computer game. That is a rare event here; Larry's clientele, while marginalized, have a strong sense of decorum. What was truly interesting about the event, though, happened shortly afterward. Dag said, "Mr. M.! Andy! Come here and check this out—" There, amid the platonic corn-and-spaghetti forms on the carpet were about thirty semidigested gelatin capsules. "Well, well. If *this* doesn't count as a square on life's bingo card, I don't know *what* does. Andrew, alert the paramedics."

That was two hours ago, and after the testosteronal posturing of chatting with the paramedics and showing off medical knowledge ("Gosh," says Dag, "some Ringer's solution, perhaps?"), we are now receiving the history of Mr. M.'s love life – a charming, saved-for-the-wedding-night affair, replete with chaste first, second, and third dates, almost instant marriages, and too many children shortly afterward.

"What about the date you *didn't* marry?" I ask.

"She stole my car. A Ford. Gold. If she hadn't done that, I probably would have married her, too. I didn't know much about selectivity then. I just remember jerking off under my desk ten times a day and thinking how insulted a date must

---

Air Family: Describes the false sense of community experienced among coworkers in an office environment.

feel if the date didn't lead to marriage. I was lonely; it was Alberta. We didn't have MTV then."

Claire and I met Mr. and Mrs. M., "Phil 'n' Irene," one delicious day months ago when we looked over the fence and were assaulted by miasmic wafts of smoke and a happy holler from Mr. M. wearing a DINNER'S ON apron. We were promptly invited over and had canned soda and "Ireneburgers" thrust into our mitts. Jolly good fun. And just before Mr. M. came outside with his ukulele, Claire whispered to me, "Andy, I sense the high probability of a chinchilla hutch on the side stoop of the house." (Chinchilla Breeders Eat Steak!)

To this day, Claire and I are just waiting to be taken aside by Irene for a hushed devotional talking-to about the lines of cosmetic products she represents and stockpiles in her garage like so many thousand unwanted, non-give-away-able kittens. "Honey, my elbows were like *pine bark* before I tried this stuff."

The two of them are sweet. They're of the generation that believes that steak houses should be dimly lit and frostily chilled (hell, they actually believe in *steak houses*). Mr. M.'s nose bears a pale spider's web film of veins, of the sort that Las Palmas housewives are currently paying good money to have sclerotherapied away from the backs of their legs. Irene *smokes*. They both wear sportswear purchased at discount houses – they discovered their bodies too late in life. They were raised to ignore their bodies and that's a little sad. But it's better than no discovery at all. They're soothing.

In our mind's eye, Irene and Phil live in a permanent 1950s. They still believe in a greeting card future. It is *their* oversize brandy snifter filled with matchbooks that I think of

when I make oversize-brandy-snifter-filled-with-matchbook jokes. This snifter rests atop their living-room table, a genetic parking lot of framed MacArthur descendant photos, mainly grandchildren, disproportionately hair do'ed in the style of Farrah, squinting with new contact lenses and looking somehow slated for bizarre deaths. Claire once peeked at a letter that was lying on a side table, and she remembered reading a phrase complaining that the jaws of life took two-and-a-half hours to reach a MacArthur descendant impaled inside an overturned tractor.

We tolerate Irene and Phil's mild racist quirks and planet-destroying peccadilloes ("I could never own any car smaller than my Cutlass *Supreme*") because their existence acts as a tranquilizer in an otherwise slightly-out-of-control world. "Sometimes," says Dag, "I have a real problem remembering if a celebrity is dead or not. But then I realize it doesn't really matter. Not to sound ghoulish, but that's sort of the way I feel about Irene and Phil – *but in the best sense of the meaning*, of course."

Anyhow—

Mr. M. starts off a joke for Dag's and my amusement: "This'll slay you. There are these three old Jewish guys sitting on a beach in Florida – (racial slur this time) – They're talking, and one of the guys asks another one, *'So where'd you get the dough to come down to retire in Florida?'* and the guy replies, *'Well, there was a fire down at the factory. A very sad affair, but fortunately I was covered by fire insurance.'*

"Fine. So then he asks the other guy where *he* got the money to come down and retire in Miami Beach, and the

---

Squirming: Discomfort inflicted on young people by old people who see no irony in their gestures. *Karen died a thousand deaths as her father made a big show of tasting a recently manufactured bottle of wine before allowing it to be poured as the family sat in Steak Hut.*

second guy replies, '*Funny, but just like my friend here, there was also a fire down at my factory as well. Praise God, I was insured.*'"

At this point Dag laughs out loud and Mr. M.'s joke-telling rhythm is thrown off, and his left hand, which is wiping the inside of a beer stein with a threadbare Birds of Arizona dishrag, stops moving. "Hey, Dag," says Mr. M.

"Yeah?"

"How come you always laugh at my jokes before I even get to the punch line?"

"Excuse me?"

"Just like I said. You always start snickering halfway through my jokes, like you were laughing *at* me instead of *with* me.' He starts drying the glass again.

"Hey, Mr. M., I'm not laughing *at* you. It's your *gestures* that are funny – your *facial* expression. You've got a pro's timing. You're a laugh riot."

Mr. MacArthur buys this. "Okay, but don't treat me like a talking seal, okay? Respect my trip. I'm a person and I pay your paycheck, too." (He says this last comment as though Dag were a total prisoner of this colorful but dead-end McJob.)

"Now where were we? Oh yeah, so the two guys turn to the guy that's been asking the questions and they say to him, '*Well what about you? Where'd you get the money to come down*

Recreational Slumming: The practice of participating in recreational activities of a class one perceives as lower than one's own: *"Karen! Donald! Let's go bowling tonight! And don't worry about shoes . . . apparently you can rent them."*

Conversational Slumming: The self-conscious enjoyment of a given conversation precisely for its lack of intellectual rigor. A major spin-off activity of *Recreational Slumming*.

Occupational Slumming: Taking a job well beneath one's skill or education level as a means of retreat from adult responsibilities and/or avoiding possible failure in one's true occupation.

and retire here in Florida?' And he replies, *'Just like with you guys there was a disaster at my place, too. There was a flood and the whole place got wiped out. Fortunately, of course, there was insurance.'*

"The two guys look really confused, then one of them says to the third guy, *'I got just one question for you. How'd you arrange a flood?'*"

Groans. Mr. M. seems pleased. He walks along the bar counter's length, the surface of which, like the narrow horseshoe of flooring surrounding the toilet of an alcoholic, is a lunar surface of leprotic cigarette burn sores. He crosses *Fiesta*-patterned purple-and-orange Orlon carpeting, scented cinnamon with BarGuard deodorant, and locks the front door. Dag delivers me a glance. Meaning? *I really must be a bit more careful with snickers in the future.* But I can see that, like myself, Dag is torn between smugly cherishing the bizarre joke-telling remnants of Mr. MacArthur's era, and the desolation of living in a future civilization cluttered with sullen, aura-free unfunny yuppies and depopulated of Bob Hope jokes.

"We might as well enjoy them while they're still around, Andy," he says. "Hey. Let's go now. Maybe Claire's in a better mood."

The Saab won't start. It alternates tubercular hacking salvos with confused bunny coughs, giving the impression of a small child blending fits of demonic possession with the coughing up of bits of hamburger. A motel guest lodging close to Larry's parking lot is yelling *fuck off* from a rear window, but his rancor is not going to ruin this wonderful desert night for us as

---

Anti-victim Device (AVD): A small fashion accessory worn on an otherwise conservative outfit which announces to the world that one still has a spark of individuality burning inside: *1940s retro ties and earrings (on men), feminist buttons, noserings (women), and the now almost completely extinct teeny weeny "rattail" haircut (both sexes).*

we're forced to walk home yet again. The smooth cool air flows over my skin like dry porcelain silt, and the too-steep mountains are amber tinted like an underwater photo of the *Andrea Doria*. There is so little pollution that perspective is warped; the mountains want to smash themselves into my face.

Baby magnesium flare twinkle lights gird the sentinel palms of Highway 111. Their skirts rustle, letting in fresh air for the countless lightly dozing birds, rats, and bougainvillea tendrils buried inside.

We peek into shop windows that hawk fluorescent swimwear, date samplers, awful abstract paintings that look like roadkill covered in sparkles. I see hats and gems and pies – such lovely loot, begging for attention like a child who doesn't want to go to bed yet. I want to slit open my stomach and rip out my eyes and cram these sights inside me. Earth.

"We resemble either the idiot twins of an Indiana car dealer tonight," says Dag of our supercool Bob Hope Golf Classic robin's-egg-blue windbreakers with white sun hats, "or a pair of drifters – with profane and murderous thoughts in our hearts. Take your pick."

"I think we look like nebbishes, myself, Dag."

Highway 111 (also known as Palm Canyon Drive) is the town's main drag and surprisingly empty tonight. A few ambisexual blondes from Orange County float vacuously back and forth in high-end Volkswagens, while skinhead marines in dented El Caminos make cruising, hustler's screeches but never stop. It's still a car culture town here, and on a busy night it can feel, as Dag so aptly phrases it, "like a Daytona, big tits, burger-and-shake kind of place where kids in go-go boots and asbestos jackets eat Death Fries in orange vinyl restaurant booths shaped like a whitewall GT tire."

We turn a corner and walk some more.

"Imagine, Andrew: 48 hours ago little Dagster here was in Nevada," he continues, now seating himself on the trunk of a dazzlingly expensive racing green Aston Martin convertible, lighting a filter-tipped cigarette. "Imagine that."

We're off the main drag now, on an unlit side street where Dag's expensive "seat" is stupidly parked. In the Aston Martin's back area are cardboard boxes loaded with papers, clothing, and junk, like an accountant's garage sale. It looks as though someone were planning to split town in an awful hurry. Not unlikely in *this* burg.

"I spent the night in a little mom-and-pop motel in the middle of nowhere. The walls had knotty pine paneling and fifties lamps and prints of deer on the wall—"

"Dag, get off the car. I feel really uncomfortable here."

"—and there was the smell of those little pink bars of motel soaps. God, I love the smell of those little things. So transient."

I'm horrified: Dag is burning holes in the roof of the car with the cherry of his cigarette. "Dag! What are you doing – cut that out! Not *again*."

"Andrew, keep your *voice* down. Please. Where *is* your cool?"

"Dag, this is too much for me. I've got to go. " I start walking away.

Dag, as I have said, is a vandal. I try to understand his behavior but fail; last week's scraping of the Cutlass Supreme was merely one incident in a long strand of such events. He seems to confine himself exclusively to vehicles bearing bumper stickers he finds repugnant. Sure enough, an inspection of this car's rear reveals a sticker saying ASK ME ABOUT MY GRANDCHILDREN.

"Come back here, Palmer. I'll stop. In a second. And besides, I want to tell you a secret."

I pause.

"It's a secret about my future," he says. Against my better judgment, I return.

"That is so *stu*pid, burning holes like that, Dag."

"Chill, boy. This sort of thing's a misdemeanor. Statute 594, California penal code. Slap on the wrist. And besides, no one's looking."

He brushes a small divot of ash away from a cigarette hole. "I want to own a hotel down in Baja, California. And I think I'm closer than you think to actually doing so."

"What?"

"That's what I want to do in my future. Own a hotel."

"Great. Now let's go."

"No," he lights up another cigarette, "not until I describe my hotel to you."

"Just *hurry*."

"I want to open a place down in San Felipe. It's on the east side of the Baja needle. It's a tiny shrimping village surrounded by nothing but sand, abandoned uranium mines, and pelicans. I'd open up a small place for friends and eccentrics only, and for staff I'd only hire elderly Mexican women and stunningly beautiful surfer and hippie type boys and girls who have had their brains swiss-cheesed from too much dope. There'd be a bar there, where everyone staples business cards and money to the walls and the ceiling, and the only light would be from ten watt bulbs hidden behind cactus skeletons on the ceiling. We'd spend nights washing zinc salves from each other's noses, drinking rum drinks, and telling stories. People who told good stories could stay for free. You wouldn't be allowed to use the bathroom unless you felt-penned a funny joke on the wall. And all of the rooms would be walled in knotty pine wood, and, as a souvenir, everyone would receive just a little bar of soap."

I have to admit, Dag's hotel sounds enchanting, but I also want to leave. "That's great, Dag. I mean, your idea really *is* great, but let's split now, all right?"

"I suppose. I—" He looks down at where he has been burning a cigarette hole while I was turned away. "Uh oh—"

"What happened?"

"Oh, shit."

The cherry from the cigarette has fallen off, and onto a box of papers and mixed junk in the car. Dag hops off the car and we both stare transfixed as the red hot little poker tip burns through a few newspaper pages, gives the impression of disappearing, then suddenly goes *whoooof!* as the box combusts as fast as a dog's bark, illuminating our horrified faces with its instant yellow mock cheer.

"Oh, God!"

"Ditch!"

I'm already gone. The two of us scram down the road, heart-in-throat, turning around only once we are two blocks away, then only briefly, to see a worst-case scenario of the Aston Martin engulfed in fizzy raspberry lava flames in a toasty, kindling ecstasy, dripping onto the road.

"Shit, Bellinghausen, this is the stupidest effing stunt you've ever pulled," and we're off running again, me ahead of Dag, my aerobic training paying off.

Dag rounds a corner behind me when I hear a muffled voice and a thump. I turn around and I see Dag bumping into the Skipper of all people, a Morongo Valley hobo type from up-valley who sometimes hangs out at Larry's (so named for the TV sitcom ship's captain hat he wears).

"Hi, Dag. Bar closed?"

"Hi, Skip. You bet. Hot date. Gotta dash," he says, already edging away and pointing his finger at the Skipper like a yuppie insincerely promising to do lunch.

Ten Texas blocks away we stop exhausted, winded, and making breathless, earth-scraping salaams. "*No one* finds out about this little blip, Andrew. Got that? No one. Not even Claire."

"Do I look brain dead? God."

Puff, puff puff.

"What about the Skipper," I asked, "think he'll put two and two together?"

"Him? *Naah*. His brain turned to carburetor gunk years ago."

"You sure?"

"Yeah." Our breath returns.

"Quick. Name ten dead redheads," commands Dag.

"What?"

"You have five seconds. One. Two. Three—"

I figure it out. "George Washington, Danny Kaye—"

"He's not dead."

"Is, too."

"Fair enough. Bonus points for you."

The remaining walk home is less funny.

I AM NOT
JEALOUS

Apparently Elvissa rode the pooch this afternoon after leaving our pool (hipster codeword: *rode the Greyhound bus*). She traveled four hours northwest to the coast at Santa Barbara to start a new job, get *this*, as a gardener at a nunnery. We're floored, really *floored* by this little chunk of news. ¶"Well," Claire fudges, "it's not really a nunnery, per se. The women wear these baggy charcoal cassocks – so Japanese! – and they cut their hair short. I saw it in the brochure. And anyhow, she's only *gardening*." ¶"Bro*chure?*" More horror. ¶"Well, the gatefolded pizza flyer thing they sent to Elvissa with her letter of acceptance." (Good God—) "She found the job on a local parish bulletin board; she says she wants to clean out her head. But I suspect that maybe she thinks Curtis could drift through there, and she wants to be around when that happens. That woman is so *good* at keeping things secret that she wants to." ¶We're now sitting in my kitchen, lolling about on burned-pine bar stools with dog-chewed legs and purple diamond-tufted tops. These are chairs that I lugged away gratis from a somewhat bitter condominium repossession sale over on Palo Fiero Road last month. ¶For atmosphere Dag has placed a cheesy red light bulb in the table counter's light socket and he's mixing dreadful drinks with dreadful names that he learned from the invading teens of last spring's break. (Date Rapes, Chemotherapies, Headless Prom Queens – who *invents* these things?)

The evening's dress code is bedtime story outfits: Claire in her flannel housecoat trimmed with a lace of cigarette burn holes, Dag in his "Lord Tyrone" burgundy rayon pyjamas with "regal" simugold drawstrings, and me in a limp plaid shirt with long johns. We look hodgepodge, rainy day and silly. "We really *must* get our fashion act together," Claire says.

"After the revolution, Claire. After the revolution," replies Dag.

Claire puts scientifically enhanced popcorn in the microwave oven. "I never feel like I'm putting food in one of these things," she then says, entering with beeps, the time-set into the LED, "it feels more like I'm inserting fuel rods into a core." She slams the door hard.

"Hey, *watch* it," I call.

"Sorry, Andy. But I'm upset. You just have no *idea* how hard it is for me to find same-sex friends. My friends have always been guys. Girls are always so froufrou. They always see me as a threat. I finally find a decent friend here in town and

---

Nutritional Slumming: Food whose enjoyment stems not from flavor but from a complex mixture of class connotations nostalgia signals, and packaging semiotics: *Katie and I bought this tub of Multi-Whip instead of real whip cream because we thought petroleum distillate whip topping seemed like the sort of food that air force wives stationed in Pensacola back in the early sixties would feed their husbands to celebrate a career promotion.*

Tele-parablizing: Morals used in everyday life that derive from TV sitcom plots: *"That's just like the episode where Jan lost her glasses!"*

she leaves on the same day as my life's grand obsession ditches me. Just bear with me, okay?"

"And that's why you were so draggy at the pool today?"

"Yes. She told me to keep the news of her going a secret. She de*tests* good-byes."

Dag seems preoccupied about the nunnery. "It'll never work," he says. "It's too Madonna/whore. I don't buy it."

"It's not something you *buy*, Dag. You sound like Tobias when you talk like that. And she's *hardly* making a vocation of 'nunning' – stop being so negative. Give her a chance." Claire resumes her perch on the stool. "Besides, would you rather she was still here in Palm Springs doing whatever *it* was she was doing? Would you like to go down to Vons supermarket and buy needle bleach with her in a year or so? Or play match-maker, perhaps – fix her up with a dental conventioneer so she can become a Palo Alto homemaker?"

The first kernel pops and it dawns on me that Dag is not only feeling rebuffed by Elvissa, but he's envious of her decision to change and reduce her life as well.

"She's renounced all of her worldly goods, I take it then," says Dag.

"I guess her roommates will filch most of her possessions she's leaving behind here in Palm Springs, poor things. VSTP: very severe taste problem, that lady. Snoopy lamps and decoupage, mostly."

"I give her three months."

Under a fusillade of popping kernels, Claire raises her voice: "I'm not going to harp on about this, Dag, but cliché or doomed as her impulse for self-betterment may be, you just can't mock it. *You* of all people. Good Lord. *You* should

---

QFD: Quelle fucking drag. "Jamie got stuck at some airport for thirty-six hours and it was, like, totally QFD."

QFM: Quelle fashion mistake. *"It was really QFM, I mean painter pants? That's 1979 beyond belief."*

understand what it means to try and get rid of all the crap in your life. But Elvissa's gone one further than you, now, *hasn't* she? She's at the next level. You're hanging on still, even though your job-job and the big city are gone – hanging on to your car and your cigarettes and your long-distance phone calls and the cocktails and the *attitude*. You still want control. What *she's* doing is no sillier than your going into a monastery, and Lord knows we've listened to your talk about *that* enough times."

The corn appropriately stops popping, and Dag stares at his feet. He gazes at them like they were two keys on a key chain but he can't remember what locks they belong to. "God. You're right. I don't believe myself. You know what I feel like? I feel like I'm twelve years old and back in Ontario and I've just sloshed gasoline all over the car and my clothing *again* – I feel like such a total dirt bag."

"Don't be a *dirt bag*, Bellinghausen. Just close your eyes," Claire says. "Close your eyes and look closely at what you've spilled. *Smell the future*."

The red light bulb was fun but tiring. We head into my room now for bedtime stories. The fireplace is lit, with the dogs snogging away blissfully atop their oval braid rug. On top of my bed's Hudson Bay blankets we eat the popcorn and feel a rare coziness amid the beeswax yellow shadows that oscillate on the wooden walls that are hung with my objects: fishing lures, sun hats, a violin, date fronds, yellowing newspapers, bead belts, rope, oxford shoes, and maps. Simple objects for a noncomplex life.

Claire starts.

L E A V E
Y O U R
B O D Y

"There was once this poor little rich girl named Linda. She was heiress to a vast family fortune, the seeds of which sprouted in slave trading in Georgia, that propagated into the Yankee textile mills of Massachusetts and Connecticut, dispersed westward into the steel mills of the Monongahela River in Pennsylvania, and ultimately bore sturdy offspring of newspapers, film, and aerospace in California. ¶"But while Linda's family's money always managed to grow and adapt to its times, Linda's family did not. It shrank, dwindled, and inbred to the point where all that remained was Linda and her mother, Doris. Linda lived in a stone mansion on a rural Delaware estate, but her mother only filed her tax claims out of the Delaware address. She hadn't even visited it in many years – she was a socialite; she lived in Paris; she was *on the jet*. If she *had* visited, she might have been able to prevent what happened to Linda. ¶"You see, Linda grew up happy as any little rich girl can, an only child in a nursery on the top floor of the stone mansion where her father read stories to her every night as she sat on his lap. Up near the ceiling, dozens of small tame canaries swirled and sang, sometimes descending to sit on their shoulders and always inspecting the lovely foods the maids would deliver. ¶"But one day her father stopped coming and he never returned. For a while, her mother occasionally came to try and read stories, but it was never the same – she had cocktails on her breath; she would cry; she swatted the birds when they came near her and after a while the birds stopped trying.

"Time passed, and in her late teens and early twenties, Linda became a beautiful but desperately unhappy woman, constantly searching for one person, one idea, or one place that could rescue her from her, well, her *life*. Linda felt charmed but targetless – utterly alone. And she had mixed feelings about her chunky inheritance – guilt at not having struggled but also sometimes feelings of queenliness and entitlement that she knew could only bring bad luck upon her. She flip-flopped.

"And like all truly rich and/or beautiful and/or famous people, she was never really sure whether people were responding to the real *her*, the pinpoint of light trapped within her flesh capsule, or if they were responding merely to the lottery prize she won at birth. She was always on the alert for fakes and leeches, poetasters and quacks.

"I'll add some more about Linda here, too: she was bright. She could discuss particle physics, say – quarks and leptons, bosons and mesons – and she could tell you who really knew about the subject versus someone who had merely read a magazine article on it. She could name most flowers and she could buy all flowers. She attended Williams College and she attended drinks parties with film stars in velveteen Manhattan aeries lit by epileptic flashbulbs. She often traveled alone to Europe. In the medieval walled city of Saint-Malo on the coast of France she lived in a small room that smelled of liqueur bonbons and dust. There she read the works of Balzac and Nancy Mitford, looking for love, looking for an idea, and having sex with Australians while planning her next European destinations.

"In western Africa she visited endless floral quilts of gerbera and oxalis – otherworldly fields where psychedelic zebras chewed tender blossoms that emerged from the barren soil overnight, borne of seeds awakened from decade-long comas by the fickle Congo rains.

"But it was in Asia, finally, where Linda found what she was looking for – high in the Himalayas amid the discarded, rusting oxygen canisters of mountaineers and the vacant, opiated, and damned bodies of Iowa sophomores – it was there she heard the idea that unlocked the mechanisms of her soul.

"She heard of a religious sect of monks and nuns in a small village who had achieved a state of saintliness – ecstasy – *release* – through a strict diet and a period of meditation that lasted for seven years, seven months, seven days, and seven hours. During this period, the saint-in-training was not allowed to speak one word or perform any other acts save those of eating, sleeping, meditation, and elimination. But it was said that the truth to be found at the end of this ordeal was *so* invariably wonderful that the suffering and denial was small change compared to the Higher contact achieved at the end.

"Unfortunately on the day of Linda's visit to the small village there was a storm. She was forced to turn back and the next day she then had to return to Delaware for a meeting with her estate lawyers. She was never able to visit the saintly village.

"Shortly thereafter she turned twenty-one. By the terms of her father's will, she then inherited the bulk of his estate. Doris, in a tense moment in a tobacco-smelling Delaware lawyer's office, learned that she would only receive a fixed but not unextravagant monthly allowance.

"Now, from her husband's estate Doris had wanted a meal; she got a snack. She was livid, and it was over this money that an irreparable rift between Linda and Doris opened up. Doris untethered herself. She became a well-upholstered, glossily lacquered citizen of money's secret world. Life became a bayeux of British health hydros, purchased Venetian bellboys who plucked the jewels from her handbag, fruitless Andean

UFO trace hunts, Lake Geneva sanatoriums and Antarctic cruises, where she would shamelessly flatter emirate princes against a backdrop of the pale blue ice of Queen Maud Land.

"And so Linda was left alone to make her decisions, and in the absence of nay-sayers, she decided to try for herself the spiritual release of the seven-year–seven-month–seven-day method.

"But in order to do this, she had to take precautions to ensure that the outside world did not impinge on her efforts. She fortified the walls of her estate, making them taller and armed with laser alarms, fearful not of robbery, but of possible interruptions. Legal documents were drawn up which ensured that such issues as taxes would be taken care of. These documents also stated the nature of her mission in advance and sat there ready to be brandished in the event that Linda's sanity might be questioned.

"Her servants she discharged, save for one retainer named Charlotte. Cars were banned from the property and the yards and gardens were let to run wild to spare the annoyances of lawn mowers. Security guards were placed on constant guard around her estate's perimeter, and another security system was hired to monitor the security guards, to prevent them from becoming lax. Nothing was to interrupt her sixteen hours a day of silent meditation.

"And thus one early March, her period of silence began.

"Immediately the yard began to return to the wild. The harsh Kentucky Blue monoculture of the lawn quickly became laced with gentler, indigenous flowers and weeds and grasses. Black-eyed Susans, forget-me-nots, cow parsley, and New Zealand flax joined the grasses that began to reclaim, soften, and punctuate the pebbled driveways and paths. The gangly,

luxurious, and painful forms of roses, thorns and their hips overtook the gazebo; wisteria strangled the porch; pyrocanthus and ivies spilled over the rockeries like soups boiling over. Small creatures moved into the yard in abundance. In summer the tips of the grass became permanently covered in a mist of sunlight sprinkled with silent, imbecilic, and amniotic butterflies, moths, and midges. Hungry raucous jays and orioles would swoop and penetrate this airy liquid. And this was Linda's world. She overlooked it from dawn to dusk from her mat on the outdoor patio, saying nothing, sharing nothing, revealing nothing.

"When fall came she would wear wool blankets given to her by Charlotte until it became too cold. Then she continued to watch her world from inside the tall glass doors of her bedroom. In winter she observed the world's dormancy; in spring she saw its renewal, and again each summer she watched its almost smothering richness of life.

"And this carried on for seven years, in which time her hair turned gray, she ceased menstruating, her skin became like a leather pulled tightly over her bones, and her voice box atrophied, making her unable to speak, even were she to want to do so.

"One day near the end of Linda's period of meditation, far away on the other side of the world in the Himalayas, a priest named Laski was reading a copy of the German magazine *Stern*, left in the local village by visiting mountaineers. In it he came across a fuzzy telephoto of a female figure, Linda,

---

Me-ism: A search by an individual, in the absence of training in traditional religious tenets, to formulate a personally tailored religion by himself. Most frequently a mishmash of reincarnation, personal dialogue with a nebulously defined god figure, naturalism, and karmic eye-for-eye attitudes.

Paper Rabies: Hypersensitivity to littering.

meditating in what looked to be a wild and rich garden. Reading the caption underneath, which described the efforts of a wealthy American heiress gone New Age, Laski felt his pulse quicken.

"Within one day Laski was on a Japan Air Lines flight into JFK airport, filled with anxiety and looking a strange sight with his steamer trunk and his robe, battling the late-afternoon crowds of Eurotrash being deposited at customs by the discount airlines and hoping that the airport limousine would take him to Linda's estate in time. So little time!

"Laski stood outside the steely gate of Linda's estate, and from within the guard's house, he heard a party in progress. Tonight, as he had correctly interpreted from the small curiosity article on Linda in the *Stern*, was to be her last night of meditation – the guards were to be released from duty and were celebrating. They were sloppy. Laski, leaving his steamer trunk outside the gate, slipped in quietly, and, without any interruption, strolled down the sunset lit remains of the driveway.

"The apple trees were filled with angry crows; blue ground spruce shrub licked at his feet; exhausted sunflowers rested their heads on broken necks while the snails gathered below like *tricoteuses*. Amid this splendor Laski stood and changed from his pale brown robe into a jacket of glimmering metal he had removed at the gate and had been carrying with him. And, after reaching Linda's house, he opened the front door, then entered the cool, dark silence that spoke to him of opulent rooms rarely used. Up a wide central staircase layered with carpet the black-red tint of pomegranate juice, Laski followed a hunch, walked through many corridors, and ended up in Linda's bedroom. Charlotte, partying with the guards, was not there to monitor his entrance.

"Then on the patio outside he saw Linda's shrunken figure gazing at the sun, which was now amber and half-descended below the horizon. Laski had arrived just in time – Linda's period of silence and meditation would be over in seconds.

"Laski looked at her body, so young still, but converted to

that of an old crone. And it could almost creak, so it seemed to him, as she turned around, revealing her face, profoundly emaciated – a terminal face like a rubber raft that has been deflated, left in the sun too long.

"She raised her body slowly, knobby and spindly, like a child's spaghetti sculpture of a graceless bird, and she shuffled across the patio and through the doors into her bedroom like a delicate breeze entering a closed room.

"She did not seem surprised to see Laski, agleam in his metal jacket. Passing by him, she pulled her lip muscles up in a satisfied smile and headed toward her bed. As she laid herself down, Laski could hear the sandpapery noises of a rough military blanket on her dress. She stared at the ceiling and Laski came to stand next to her.

"'You children from Europe . . . from America . . .' he said, 'you try so hard but you get everything wrong – you and your strange little handcarved religions you make for yourselves. Yes, you were to meditate for seven years and seven months and seven days and seven hours in my religion, but that's in *my* calendar, not yours. In *your* calendar the time comes out to just over *one* year. You went seven times longer than you had to . . . you went for far too—' but then Laski fell silent. Linda's eyes became like those he had seen that afternoon at the airport – the eyes of emigrants about to emerge through the sliding doors of customs and finally enter the new world for which they have burned all bridges.

"Yes, Linda had done everything incorrectly, but she had won anyway. It was a strange victory, but a victory nonetheless. Laski realized he had met his superior. He quickly removed the jacket of his priesthood, a jacket well over two thousand years old to which new ornaments were always being added and from which old ornaments continually decayed. Gold and platinum threads woven with yak's wool bore obsidian beads and buttons of jade. There was a ruby from Marco Polo and a 7Up bottle cap given by the first pilot to ever land in Laski's village.

"Laski took this jacket and placed it on Linda's body, now

undergoing a supernatural conversion. His gesture was accompanied by the cracking of her ribs and a breathy squeak of ecstasy. 'Poor sweet child,' he whispered as he kissed her on the forehead.

"And with this kiss, Linda's skull caved in like so many fragile green plastic berry baskets, left outside over a winter, crushing in one's hand. Yes, her skull caved in and turned to dust – and the piece of light that was truly Linda vacated her old vessel, then flitted heavenward, where it went to sit – like a small yellow bird that can sing all songs – on the right hand of her god."

GROW
FLOWERS

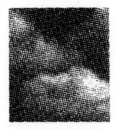

Years ago, after I first started to make a bit of money, I used to go to the local garden center every fall and purchase fifty-two daffodil bulbs. Shortly thereafter, I would then go into my parents' backyard with a deck of fifty-two wax-coated playing cards and hurl the cards across the lawn. Wherever a card fell, I would plant one of the bulbs. Of course, I could have just tossed the bulbs themselves, but the point of the matter is, I *didn't*. ¶Planting bulbs this way creates a very natural spray effect – the same silent algorithms that dictate the torque in a flock of sparrows or the gnarl of a piece of driftwood also dictate success in this formal matter, too. ¶And come spring, after the daffodils and the narcissi have spoken their delicate little haiku to the world and spilled their cold, gentle scent, their crinkly beige onion paper remnants inform us that summer will soon be here and that it is now time to mow the lawn. ¶Nothing very very good and nothing very very bad ever lasts for very very long. ¶I wake up and it's maybe 5:30 or so in the morning. The three of us are sprawled on top of the bed where we fell asleep. The dogs snooze on the floor next to the near-dead embers. Outside there is only a hint of light, the breathlessness of oleanders and no cooing of doves. I smell the warm carbon dioxide smell of sleep and enclosure. ¶These creatures here in this room with me – these are the creatures I love and who love me. Together I feel like we are a strange and forbidden garden – I feel so happy I could die. If I could have it thus, I would like this moment to continue forever.

I go back to sleep.

PART THREE

DEFINE
NORMAL

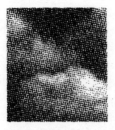

Fifteen years ago, on what remains as possibly the most unhip day of my life, my entire family, all nine of us, went to have our group portrait taken at a local photo salon. As a result of that hot and endless sitting, the nine of us spent the next fifteen years trying bravely to live up to the corn-fed optimism, the cheerful waves of shampoo, and the airbrushed teeth-beams that the resultant photo is still capable of emitting to this day. We may look dated in this photo, but we look *perfect*, too. In it, we're beaming earnestly to the right, off toward what seems to be the future but which was actually Mr. Leonard, the photographer and a lonely old widower with hair implants, holding something mysterious in his left hand and yelling, "*Fromage!*" ¶When the photo first came home, it rested gloriously for maybe one hour on top of the fireplace, placed there guilelessly by my father, who was shortly there-after pressured by a forest fire of shrill teenage voices fearful of peer mockery to remove it immediately. It was subsequently moved to a never-sat-in portion of his den, where it hangs to this day, like a forgotten pet gerbil dying of starvation. It is visited only rarely but deliberately by any one of the nine of us, in between our ups and downs in life, when we need a good dose of "but we were all so innocent once" to add that decisive literary note of melodrama to our sorrows.

Again, that was fifteen years ago. This year, however, was the year everyone in the family finally decided to stop trying to live up to that bloody photo and the shimmering but untrue promise it made to us. This is the year we decided to call it quits, normality-wise; the year we went the way families just *do*, the year everyone finally decided to be them*selves* and to hell with it. The year no one came home for Christmas. Just me and Tyler, Mom and Dad.

"Wasn't that a fabulous year, Andy? Remember?" This is my sister Deirdre on the phone, referring to the year in which the photo was taken. At the moment Deirdre's in the middle of a "heinously ugly" divorce from a cop down in Texas ("It takes me four years to discover that he's a pseudo-intimate, Andy – whatta slimeball") and her voice is rife with tricyclic antidepressants. She was the Best Looking and Most Popular of the Palmer girls; now she phones friends and relatives at 2:30 in the morning and scares them silly with idle, slightly druggy chat: "The world seemed so shiny and new then, Andy, I *know* I sound cliché. God – I'd suntan then and not be afraid of sarcomas; all it took to make me feel so alive I thought I might burst was a ride in Bobby Viljoen's Roadrunner to a party that had tons of unknown people."

Deirdre's phone calls are scary on several levels, not the least of which is that her rantings tend to be true. There really *is* something silent and dull about losing youth; youth really *is*, as Deirdre says, a sad evocative perfume built of many stray smells. The perfume of *my* youth? A pungent blend of new

---

Bradyism: A multisibling sensibility derived from having grown up in large families. A rarity in those born after approximately 1965, symptoms of *Bradyism* include a facility for mind games, emotional withdrawal in situations of overcrowding, and a deeply felt need for a well-defined personal space.

basketballs, Zamboni scrapings, and stereo wiring overheated from playing too many Supertramp albums. And, of course, the steamy halogenated brew of the Kempsey twins' Jacuzzi on a Friday night, a hot soup garnished with flakes of dead skin, aluminum beer cans, and unlucky winged insects.

I have three brothers and three sisters, and we were never a "hugging family." I, in fact, have no memory of having once been hugged by a parental unit (frankly, I'm suspicious of the practice). No, I think *psychic dodge ball* would probably better define our family dynamic. I was number five out of the seven children – the total middle child. I had to scramble harder than most siblings for any attention in our household.

The Palmer children, all seven of us, have the stalwart, sensible, and unhuggable names that our parents' generation favored – Andrew, Deirdre, Kathleen, Susan, Dave, and Evan. Tyler is *un peu* exotic, but then he *is* the love child. I once told Tyler I wanted to change my name to something new and hippie-ish, like Harmony or Dust. He looked at me: "You're *mad*. Andrew looks great on a resumé – what more could you ask for? Weirdos named Beehive or Fiber Bar *never* make middle management."

Deirdre will be in Port Arthur, Texas this Christmas, being depressed with her bad marriage made too early in life.

Dave, my oldest brother – the one who should have been the scientist but who grew a filmy pony tail instead and who now sells records in an alternative record shop in Seattle (he and his girlfriend, Rain, only wear black) – he's in London,

---

Black Holes: An X generation subgroup best known for their possession of almost entirely black wardrobes.

Black Dens: Where *Black Holes* live; often unheated warehouses with Day-Glo spray painting, mutilated mannequins, Elvis references, dozens of overflowing ashtrays, broken mirror sculptures, and Velvet Underground music playing in background.

England this Christmas, doing Ecstasy and going to nightclubs. When he comes back, he'll affect an English accent for the next six months.

Kathleen, the second eldest, is ideologically opposed to Christmas; she disapproves of most bourgeois sentimentality. She runs a lucrative feminist dairy farm up in the allergen-free belt of eastern British Columbia and says that when "the invasion" finally comes, we'll all be out shopping for greeting cards and we'll deserve everything that happens to us.

Susan, my favorite sister, the jokiest sister and the family actress, panicked after graduating from college years back, went into law, married this horrible know-everything yuppie lawyer named *Brian* (a union that can only lead to grief). Overnight she became so unnaturally serious. It can happen. I've seen it happen lots of times.

The two of them live in Chicago. On Christmas morning Brian will be taking Polaroids of their baby *Chelsea* (his name choice) in the crib which has, I believe, a Krugerrand inset in the headboard. They'll probably work all day, right through dinner.

One day I hope to retrieve Susan from her cheerless fate. Dave and I wanted to hire a deprogrammer at one point, actually going so far as to call the theology department of the university to try and find out where to locate one.

Aside from Tyler, whom you already know about, there

Strangelove Reproduction: Having children to make up for the fact that one no longer believes in the future.

Squires: The most common X generation subgroup and the only subgroup given to breeding. *Squires* exist almost exclusively in couples and are recognizable by their frantic attempts to recreate a semblance of Eisenhower-era plenitude in their daily lives in the face of exorbitant housing prices and two-job lifestyles. *Squires* tend to be continually exhausted from their voraciously acquisitive pursuit of furniture and knickknacks.

remains only Evan, in Eugene, Oregon. Neighbors call him "the normal Palmer child." But then there are things the neighbors don't know: how he drinks to excess, blows his salary on coke, how he's losing his looks almost daily, and how he will confide to Dave, Tyler, and me how he cheats on his wife, Lisa, whom he addresses in an Elmer Fudd cartoon voice in public. Evan won't eat vegetables, either, and we're all convinced that one day his heart is simply going to explode. I mean, go completely *kablooey* inside his chest. He doesn't care.

Oh, Mr. Leonard, how *did* we all end up so messy? We're looking hard for that *fromage* you were holding – we really are – but we're just *not* seeing it any more. Send us a clue, *please*.

Two days before Christmas, Palm Springs Airport is crammed with cranberry-skinned tourists and geeky scalped marines all heading home for their annual doses of slammed doors, righteously abandoned meals, and the traditional family psychodramas. Claire is crabbily chainsmoking while waiting for her flight to New York; I'm waiting for my flight to Portland. Dag is affecting an ersatz bonhomie; he doesn't want us to know how lonely he'll be for the week we're away. Even the MacArthurs are heading up to Calgary for the holidays.

Claire's crabbiness is a defense mechanism: "I *know* you guys think I'm an obsequious doormat for following Tobias to New York. Stop looking at me like that."

"Actually, Claire, I'm just reading the paper," I say.

"Well you *want* to stare at me. I can tell."

Why bother telling her she's only being paranoid? Since Tobias left that day, Claire has had only the most cursory of telephone conversations with him. She chirped away, making all sorts of plans. Tobias merely listened in at the other end like a restaurant patron being lengthily informed of the day's specials – mahimahi, flounder, swordfish – all of which he knew right from the start he didn't want.

So here we sit in the outdoor lounge area waiting for our buses with wings. My plane leaves first, and before I leave to cross the tarmac, Dag tells me to try not to burn down the house.

As mentioned before, my parents, "Frank 'n' Louise," have turned the house into a museum of fifteen years ago – the last year they ever bought new furniture and the year the Family Photo was taken. Since that time, most of their energies have been channeled into staving off evidence of time's passing.

Okay, obviously a few small tokens of cultural progression have been allowed entry into the house – small tokens such as bulk and generic grocery shopping, boxy ugly evidence of which clutters up the kitchen, evidence in which they see no embarrassment. ("I know it's a lapse in taste, pudding, but it saves so much *money*.")

There are also a few new items of technology in the house, mostly brought in on Tyler's insistence: a microwave oven, a VCR, and a telephone answering machine. In regard to this, I notice that my parents, technophobes both, will speak into the phone answering machine with all the hesitancy of a Mrs. Stuyvesant Fish making a gramophone recording for a time capsule.

Poverty Lurks: Financial paranoia instilled in offspring by depression-era parents.

Pull-the-plug, Slice the pie: A fantasy in which an offspring mentally tallies up the net worth of his parents.

Underdogging: The tendency to almost invariably side with the underdog in a given situation. The consumer expression of this trait is the purchasing of less successful, "sad," or failing products: *"I know these Vienna franks are heart failure on a stick, but they were so sad looking up against all the other yuppie food items that I just had to buy them."*

"Mom, why didn't you and Dad just go to Maui this year and give up on Christmas. Tyler and I are depressed already."

"Maybe next year, dear, when your father and I are a bit more flush. You know what prices are like. . . ."

"You say that every year. I wish you guys would stop coupon clipping. Pretending you're poor."

"Indulge us, pumpkin. We *enjoy* playing hovel."

We're pulling out of the airport in Portland and reentering the familiar drizzling greenscape of Portland. Already, after ten minutes, *any* spiritual or psychic progress I may have made in the absence of my family has vanished or been invalidated.

"So, is that the way you're cutting your hair now, dear?"

I am reminded that no matter how hard you try, you can never be more than twelve years old with your parents. Parents earnestly try not to inflame, but their comments contain no scale and a strange focus. Discussing your private life with parents is like misguidedly looking at a zit in a car's rearview mirror and being convinced, in the absence of contrast or context, that you have developed combined heat rash and skin cancer.

"So," I say, "it really *is* just me and Tyler at home this year?"

"Seems that way. But I think Dee might come up from Port Arthur. She'll be in her old bedroom soon enough. I can see the signs."

"Signs?"

Mom increases the wiper-blade speed and turns on the lights. Something's on her mind.

"Oh, you've all left and come back and left and come back so many times now, I don't really even see the point in telling my friends that my kids have left home. Not that the subject ever *comes up* these days. My friends are all going through similar things with their kids. When I bump into someone at the Safeway nowadays, it's implicit we don't ask about the children the way we used to. We'd get too depressed. Oh, by the way, you remember Allana du Bois?"

"The dish?"

"Shaved her head and joined a cult."

"No!"

"And not before she sold off all of her mother's jewelry to pay for her share of the guru's Lotus Elite. She left Post-it Notes all over the house saying, 'I'll pray for you, Mom.' Mom finally booted her out. She's growing turnips now in Tennessee."

"Everyone's such a mess. Nobody turned out normal. Have you seen anyone else?"

"Everyone. But I can't remember their names. Donny . . . Arnold . . . I remember their faces from when they used to come over to the house for Popsicles. But they all look so beaten, so *old* now – so prematurely *middle-aged*. Tyler's friends, though, I *must* say, are all so perky. They're different."

"Tyler's friends live in bubbles."

"That's neither true nor fair, Andy."

She's right. I'm just jealous of how unafraid Tyler's friends are of the future. Scared and envious. "Okay. Sorry. What were the signs that Dee might be coming home? You were saying—"

The traffic is light on Sandy Boulevard as we head toward the steel bridges downtown, bridges the color of clouds, and bridges so large and complex that they remind me of Claire's New York City. I wonder if their mass will contaminate the laws of gravity.

"Well, the moment one of you kids phones up and gets nostalgic for the past or starts talking about how poorly a job

is going, I know it's time to put out the fresh linen. Or if things are going *too well*. Three months ago Dee called and said Luke was buying her her own frozen yogurt franchise. She'd never been more excited. Right away I told your father, 'Frank, I give her till spring before she's back up in her bedroom boo-hooing over her high-school annuals.' Looks like I'll win that bet.

"Or the time Davie had the one halfway decent job he ever had, working as an art director at that magazine and telling me all the time how he loved it. Well, I knew it was only a matter of minutes before he'd become bored, and sure enough, *ding-dong*, there goes the doorbell, and there's Davie with that girl of his, *Rain*, looking like refugees from a child labor camp. The loving couple lived at the house for *six months*, Andy. You weren't here; you were in Japan or something. You have no *idea* what *that* was like. I *still* find toenail clippings everywhere. Your poor father found one in the freezer – black nail polish – *aw*ful creature."

"Do you and Rain tolerate each other now?"

"Barely. Can't say I'm unhappy to know she's in England this Christmas."

It's raining heavily now, and making one of my favorite sounds, that of rain on a car's metal roof. Mom sighs. "I really did have such high hopes for all of you kids. I mean, how can you look in your little baby's face and not feel that way? But I just had to give up caring what any of you do with your lives. I hope you don't mind, but it's made my life *that much* easier."

Pulling in the driveway, I see Tyler dashing out into his car,

---

2 + 2 = 5-ism: Caving in to a target marketing strategy aimed at oneself after holding out for a long period of time. *"Oh, all right, I'll buy your stupid cola. Now leave me alone."*

Option Paralysis: The tendency, when given unlimited choices, to make none.

protecting his artfully coifed head from the rain with his red gym bag. "Hi, Andy!" he shouts before slamming the door after entering his own warm and dry world. Through a crack in the window he cranes his neck and adds, "Welcome to the house that time forgot!"

MTV
NOT
BULLETS

Christmas Eve. ¶I am buying massive quantities of candles today, but I'm not saying why. Votive candles, birthday candles, emergency candles, dinner candles, Jewish candles, Christmas candles, and candles from the Hindu bookstore bearing peoploid cartoons of saints. They all count – all flames are equal. ¶At the Durst Thriftee Mart on 21st Street, Tyler is too embarrassed for words by this shopping compulsion; he's placed a frozen Butterball turkey in my cart to make it look more festive and less deviant. "What exactly *is* a votive candle, anyway?" asks Tyler, betraying both dizziness and a secular upbringing as he inhales deeply of the overpowering and cloying synthetic blueberry pong of a dinner candle. ¶"You light them when you say a prayer. All the churches in Europe have them." ¶"Oh. Here's one you missed." He hands me a bulbous red table candle, covered in fishnet stocking material, the sort that you find in a mom-and-pop Italian restaurant. "People sure are looking funny at your cart, Andy. I wish you'd tell me what these candles were all for." ¶"It's a yuletide surprise, Tyler. Just hang in there." We head toward the seasonally busy checkout counter, looking surprisingly normal in our semi-scruff outfits, taken from my old bedroom closet and dating from my punk days – Tyler's in an old leather jacket I picked up in Munich; I'm in beat-up layered shirts and jeans.

Outside it's raining, of course.

In Tyler's car heading back up Burnside Avenue on the way home, I attempt to tell Tyler the story Dag told about the end of the world in Vons supermarket. "I have a friend down in Palm Springs. He says that when the air raid sirens go off, the first thing people run for are the candles."

"So?"

"I think that's why people were looking at us strangely back at the Durst Thriftee Mart. They were wondering why they couldn't hear the sirens."

"Hmmm. Canned goods, too," he replies, absorbed in a copy of *Vanity Fair* (I'm driving). "You think I should bleach my hair white?"

"You're not using aluminum pots and pans still, are you, Andy?" asks my father, standing in the living room, winding up the grandfather clock. "Get rid of them, *pronto*. Dietary aluminum is your gateway to Alzheimer's disease."

Dad had a stroke two years ago. Nothing major, but he lost the use of his right hand for a week, and now he has to take this medication that makes him unable to secrete tears; to cry. I must say, the experience certainly scared him, and

he changed quite a few things in his life. Particularly his eating habits. Prior to the stroke he'd eat like a farmhand, scarfing down chunks of red meat laced with hormones and antibiotics and God knows what else, chased with mounds of mashed potato and fountains of Scotch. Now, much to my mother's relief, he eats chicken and vegetables, is a regular habitué of organic food stores, and has installed a vitamin rack in the kitchen that reeks of a hippie vitamin B stench and makes the room resemble a pharmacy.

Like Mr. MacArthur, Dad discovered his body late in life. It took him a brush with death to deprogram himself of dietary fictions invented by railroaders, cattlemen, and petrochemical and pharmaceutical firms over the centuries. But again, better late than never.

"No, Dad. No aluminum."

"Good good good." He turns and looks at the TV set across the room and then makes disparaging noises at an angry mob of protesting young men rioting somewhere in the world. "Just *look* at those guys. Don't any of them have jobs? Give them all something to do. Satellite them Tyler's rock videos – *anything* – but keep them busy. Jesus." Dad, like Dag's ex-coworker Margaret, does not believe human beings are built to deal constructively with free time.

Later on, Tyler escapes from dinner, leaving only me, Mom and Dad, the four food groups, and a predictable tension present.

Personality Tithe: A price paid for becoming a couple; previously amusing human beings become boring: *"Thanks for inviting us, but Noreen and I are going to look at flatware catalogs tonight. Afterward we're going to watch the shopping channel."*

Jack-and-Jill Party: A *Squire* tradition; baby showers to which both men and women friends are invited as opposed to only women. Doubled purchasing power of bisexual attendance brings gift values up to Eisenhower-era standards.

"Mom, I don't *want* any presents for Christmas. I don't want any *things* in my life."

"Christmas without presents? You're mad. Are you staring at the sun down there?"

Afterward, in the absence of the bulk of his children, my maudlin father flounders through the empty rooms of the house like a tanker that has punctured its hull with its own anchor, searching for a port, a place to weld shut the wound. Finally he decides to stuff the stockings by the fireplace. Into Tyler's he places treats he takes a great pleasure in buying every year: baby Listerine bottles, Japanese oranges, peanut brittle, screwdrivers, and lottery tickets. When it comes to my stocking, he asks me to leave the room even though I know he'd like my company. *I* become the one who roams the house, a house far too large for too few people. Even the Christmas tree, decorated this year by rote rather than with passion, can't cheer things up.

The phone is no friend; Portland is Deadsville at the moment. My friends are all either married, boring, and depressed; single, bored, and depressed; or moved out of town to avoid boredom and depression. And some of them have bought houses, which has to be kiss of death, personality-wise. When someone tells you they've just bought a house, they might as well tell you they no longer have a personality. You can immediately assume so many things: that they're locked into jobs they hate; that they're broke; that they spend every night watching videos; that they're fifteen pounds overweight; that they no longer listen to new ideas. It's profoundly depressing. And the *worst* part of it is that people in their houses don't even *like* where they're living. What few happy moments they possess are those gleaned from dreams of *upgrading*.

God, where did my grouchy mood come from?

The world has become one great big quiet house like Deirdre's house in Texas. Life doesn't *have* to be this way.

Earlier on I made the mistake of complaining about the house's lack of amusement and my Dad joked, "Don't make us mad, or we'll move into a condo with no guest room and no linen the way all of your friends' parents did." He thought he was making a real yuck.

Right.

As if they would move. I know they never will. They will battle the forces of change; they will manufacture talismans against it, talismans like the paper fire logs Mom makes from rolled-up newspapers. They will putter away inside the house until the future, like a horrible diseased drifter, breaks its way inside and commits an atrocity in the form of death or disease or fire or (this is what they *really* fear) *bankruptcy*. The drifter's visit will jolt them out of complacency; it will validate their anxiety. They know his dreadful arrival is inevitable, and they can see this drifter's purulent green lesions the color of hospital walls, his wardrobe chosen at random from bins at the back of the Boys and Girls Club of America depot in Santa Monica, where he also sleeps at night. And they know that he owns no land and that he won't discuss TV and that he'll trap the sparrows inside the birdhouse with duct tape.

But they won't talk about him.

By eleven, Mom and Dad are both asleep and Tyler is out partying. A brief phone call from Dag reassures me that life exists elsewhere in the universe. Hot news for the day was the Aston Martin fire making page seven of the *Desert Sun* (more than a hundred thousand dollars damage, raising the crime to a felony level), and the Skipper showing up for drinks at Larry's, ordering up a storm, then walking out when Dag

---

Down-nesting: The tendency of parents to move to smaller, guest-room-free houses after the children have moved away so as to avoid children aged 20 to 30 who have boomeranged home.

Homeowner Envy: Feelings of jealousy generated in the young and the disenfranchised when facing gruesome housing statistics.

asked him to pay the bill. Dag stupidly let him get away with it. I think we're in for trouble.

"Oh yes. My brother the jingle writer sent me an old parachute to wrap the Saab up in at night. Some gift, eh?"

Later on, I inhale a box of chocolate Lu cookies while watching cable TV. Even later, going in to putz about the kitchen, I realize that I am so bored I think I'm going to faint. This was not a good idea coming home for Christmas. I'm too old. Years ago, coming back from schools or trips, I always expected some sort of new perspective or fresh insight about the family on returning. That doesn't happen any more – the days of revelation about my parents, at least, are over. I'm left with two nice people, mind you, more than most people get, but it's time to move on. I think we'd all appreciate that.

LESS
IS A
POSSIBILITY

TRANS
FORM

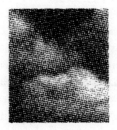

Christmas Day. ¶Since early this morning I have been in the living room with my candles – hundreds, possibly thousands of them – as well as rolls and rolls of angry, rattling tinfoil and stacks of disposable pie plates. I've been placing candles on every flat surface available, the foils not only protecting surfaces from dribbling wax but serving as well to double the candle flames via reflection. ¶Candles are everywhere: on the piano, on the bookshelves, on the coffee table, on the mantelpiece, in the fireplace, on the windowsill guarding against the par-for-the-course dismal dark wet gloss of weather. On top of the oak stereo console alone, there must be at least fifty candles, an Esperanto family portrait of all heights and levels. Syndicated cartoon characters rest amid silver swirls, spokes of lemon and lime colour. There are colonnades of raspberry and glades of white – a motley grid-lock demonstrator mix for someone who's never before seen a candle. ¶I hear the sound of taps running upstairs and my Dad calls down, "Andy, is that you down there?" ¶"Merry Christmas, Dad. Everyone up yet?" ¶"Almost. Your mother's slugging Tyler in the stomach as we speak. What are you doing down there?" ¶"It's a surprise. Promise me something. Promise that you won't come down for fifteen minutes. That's all I need – fifteen minutes."

"Don't worry. It'll take his Highness at least that long to decide between gel and mousse."

"You promise then?"

"Fifteen minutes and ticking."

Have you ever tried to light thousands of candles? It takes longer than you think. Using a simple white dinner candle as a punk, with a dish underneath to collect the drippings, I light my babies' wicks – my grids of votives, platoons of *yahrzeits* and occasional rogue sand candles. I light them all, and I can feel the room heating up. A window has to be opened to allow oxygen and cold winds into the room. I finish.

Soon the three resident Palmer family members assemble at the top of the stairs. "All set, Andy. We're coming down," calls my Dad, assisted by the percussion of Tyler's feet clomping down the stairs and his background vocals of "*new skis, new skis, new skis, new skis . . .*"

Mom mentions that she smells wax, but her voice trails off quickly. I can see that they have rounded the corner and can see and feel the buttery yellow pressure of flames dancing outward from the living-room door. They round the corner.

"Oh, *my*—" says Mom, as the three of them enter the room, speechless, turning in slow circles, seeing the normally dreary living room covered with a molten living cake-icing of white fire, all surfaces devoured in flame – a dazzling fleeting empire of ideal light. All of us are instantaneously disembodied from the vulgarities of gravity; we enter a realm in which all bodies can perform acrobatics like an astronaut in orbit, cheered on by febrile, licking shadows.

"It's like *Paris* . . ." says Dad, referring, I'm sure, to Notre Dame cathedral as he inhales the air – hot and slightly singed, the way air must smell, say, after a UFO leaves a circular scorchburn in a wheat field.

I'm looking at the results of my production, too. In my

head I'm reinventing this old space in its burst of chrome yellow. The effect is more than even I'd considered; this light is painlessly and without rancor burning acetylene holes in my forehead and plucking me out from my body. This light is also making the eyes of my family burn, if only momentarily, with the possibilities of existence in our time.

"Oh, Andy," says my mother, sitting down. "Do you know what this is like? It's like the dream everyone gets sometimes – the one where you're in your house and you suddenly discover a new room that you never knew was there. But once you've seen the room you say to yourself, '*Oh, how obvious – of course that room is there. It always has been.*'"

Tyler and Dad sit down, with the pleasing clumsiness of jackpot lottery winners. "It's a video, Andy," says Tyler, "a total *video.*"

But there is a problem.

Later on life reverts to normal. The candles slowly snuff themselves out and normal morning life resumes. Mom goes to fetch a pot of coffee; Dad deactivates the actinium heart of the smoke detectors to preclude a sonic disaster; Tyler loots his stocking and demolishes his gifts. ("New skis! I can die now!")

But I get this feeling—

It is a feeling that our emotions, while wonderful, are transpiring in a vacuum, and I think it boils down to the fact that we're middle class.

You see, when you're middle class, you have to live with the fact that history will ignore you. You have to live with the fact that history can never champion your causes and that history will never feel sorry for you. It is the price that is paid for day-to-day comfort and silence. And because of this price, all happinesses are sterile; all sadnesses go unpitied.

And any small moments of intense, flaring beauty such as this morning's will be utterly forgotten, dissolved by time like a super-8 film left out in the rain, without sound, and quickly replaced by thousands of silently growing trees.

WELCOME
HOME FROM
VIETNAM, SON

Time to escape. I want my real life back with all of its funny smells, pockets of loneliness, and long, clear car rides. I want my friends and my dopey job dispensing cocktails to leftovers. I miss heat and dryness and light. ¶"You're *okay* down there in Palm Springs, aren't you?" asks Tyler two days later as we roar up the mountain to visit the Vietnam memorial en route to the airport. ¶"Alright, Tyler – *spill*. What have Mom and Dad been saying?" ¶"Nothing. They just sigh a lot. But they don't sigh over you *nearly* as much as they do about Dee or Davie." ¶"Oh?" ¶"What do you *do* down there, anyway? You don't have a TV. You don't have any friends—" ¶"I do, *too*, have friends, Tyler." ¶"Okay, so you have friends. But I worry about you. That's all. You seem like you're only skimming the surface of life, like a water spider – like you have some secret that prevents you from entering the mundane everyday world. *And that's fine* – but it scares me. If you, oh, I don't know, disappeared or something, I don't know that I could deal with it." ¶"God, Tyler. I'm not going anywhere. I promise. Chill, okay? Park over there—" ¶"You promise to give me a bit of warning? I mean, if you're going to leave or metamorphose or whatever it is you're planning to do—" ¶"Stop being so grisly. Yeah, sure, I promise." ¶*Just don't leave me behind.* That's all. I know – it looks as if I enjoy what's going on with my life and everything, but listen, my heart's only half in it. You give my friends and me a bum rap but I'd give *all* of this up in a *flash* if someone had an even remotely plausible alternative."

"Tyler, *stop.*"

"I just get so *sick* of being jealous of everything, Andy—" There's no stopping the boy. "—And it scares me that I don't see a future. And I don't understand this reflex of mine to be such a smartass about everything. It *really* scares me. I may not look like I'm paying any attention to anything, Andy, but I am. But I can't allow myself to show it. And I don't know why."

Walking up the hill to the memorial's entrance, I wonder what all *that* was about. I guess I'm going to have to be (as Claire says) "just a teentsy bit more jolly about things." But it's hard.

At Brookings they hauled 800,000 pounds of fish across the docks and in Klamath Falls there was a fine show of Aberdeen Angus Cattle. And Oregon was indeed a land of honey, the state licensing 2,000 beekeepers in 1964.

The Vietnam memorial is called A Garden of Solace. It is a Guggenheim-like helix carved and bridged into a mountain slope that resembles mounds of emeralds sprayed with a vegetable mister. Visitors start at the bottom of a coiled pathway that proceeds upward and read from a series of stone blocks bearing carved text that tells of the escalating events of the Vietnam War in contrast with daily life back home in Oregon.

Derision Preemption: A life-style tactic; the refusal to go out on any sort of emotional limb so as to avoid mockery from peers. *Derision Preemption is* the main goal of *Knee-Jerk Irony.*

Below these juxtaposed narratives are carved the names of brushcut Oregon boys who died in foreign mud.

The site is both a remarkable document and an enchanted space. All year round, one finds sojourners and mourners of all ages and appearance in various stages of psychic disintegration, reconstruction, and reintegration, leaving in their wake small clusters of flowers, letters, and drawings, often in a shaky childlike scrawl and, of course, tears.

Tyler displays a modicum of respect on this visit, that is to say, he doesn't break out into spontaneous fits of song and dance as he might were we to be at the Clackamas County Mall. His earlier outburst is over and will never, I am quite confident, ever be alluded to again. "Andy. I don't *get* it. I mean, this is a cool enough place and all, but why should you be interested in Vietnam. It was over before you'd even reached puberty."

"I'm hardly an expert on the subject, Tyler, but I *do* remember a bit of it. Faint stuff; black-and-white TV stuff. Growing up, Vietnam was a background color in life, like red or blue or gold – it tinted everything. And then suddenly one day it just disappeared. Imagine that one morning you woke up and suddenly the color green had vanished. I come here to see a color that I can't see anywhere else any more."

"Well *I* can't remember any of it."

"You wouldn't want to. They were ugly times—"

Green Division: To know the difference between envy and jealousy.

Knee-Jerk Irony: The tendency to make flippant ironic comments as a reflexive matter of course in everyday conversation.

Fame-induced Apathy: The attitude that no activity is worth pursuing unless one can become very famous pursuing it. *Fame-induced Apathy* mimics laziness, but its roots are much deeper.

I exit Tyler's questioning.

Okay, *yes*, I think to myself, they *were* ugly times. But they were also the only times I'll ever get – genuine capital H history times, before *history* was turned into a press release, a marketing strategy, and a cynical campaign tool. And *hey*, it's not as if I got to see much real history, either – I arrived to see a concert in history's arena just as the final set was finishing. But I saw enough, and today, in the bizarre absence of all time cues, I need a connection to a past of some importance, however wan the connection.

I blink, as though exiting a trance. "Hey, Tyler – you all set to take me to the airport? Flight 1313 to Stupidville should be leaving soon."

The flight hub's in Phoenix, and a few hours later, back in the desert I cab home from the airport as Dag is at work and Claire is still in New York.

The sky is a dreamy tropical black velvet. Swooning but-terfly palms bend to tell the full moon a filthy farmer's daughter joke. The dry air squeaks of pollen's gossipy promis-cuity, and a recently trimmed Ponderosa lemon tree nearby smells cleaner than anything I've ever smelled before. Astringent. The absence of doggies tells me that Dag's let them out to prowl.

Outside of the little swinging wrought-iron gate of the

NOSTALGIA
IS
A
WEAPON

courtyard that connects all of our bungalows, I leave my luggage and walk inside. Like a game-show host welcoming a new contestant, I say, *"Hello, doors!"* to both Claire's and Dag's front doors. Then I walk over to my own door, behind which I can hear my telephone starting to ring. But this doesn't prevent me from giving my front door a little kiss. I mean wouldn't *you?*

ADVENTURE
WITHOUT RISK
IS DISNEYLAND

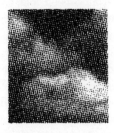

Claire's on the phone from New York with a note of confidence in her voice that's never been there before – more italics than usual. After minor holiday pleasantries, I get to the point and ask the Big Question: "How'd things work out with Tobias?" ¶"*Comme çi, comme ça.* This calls for a cigarette, Lambiekins – hang on – there should be one in this case here. *Bulgari*, get *that*. Mom's new husband Armand is just loa*ded*. He owns the marketing rights to those two little buttons on push-button telephones – the star and the zero. That's like owning the marketing rights to the *moon*. Can you bear it?" I hear a click click as she lights one of Armand's pilfered Sobranies. "Yes. Tobias. Well well. What a case." A long inhale. ¶Silence. ¶Exhale. ¶I probe: "When did you finally see him?" ¶"Today. Can you believe it? Five *days* after Christmas. Unbelievable. I'd made all these plans to meet before, but he kept breaking them, the knob. Finally we were going to meet down in Soho for lunch, in spite of the fact that I felt like a pig-bag after partying with Allan and his buddies the night before. I even managed to arrive down in Soho early – only to discover that the restaurant had closed down. Bloody condos, they're ruining *everything*.

You wouldn't believe Soho now, Andy. It's like a Disney theme park, except with better haircuts and souvenirs. Everyone has an IQ of 110 but lords it up like it's 140 and every second person on the street is Japanese and carrying around Andy Warhol and Roy Lichtenstein prints that are worth their weight in uranium. And everyone looks so pleased with themselves."

"But what about Tobias?"

"Yeah yeah yeah. So I'm early. And it is c-o-l-d out, Andy. Shocking cold; break-your-ears-off cold, and so I have to spend longer than normal in stores looking at junk I'd never give one nanosecond's worth of time to normally – all just to stay warm. So anyhow, I'm in this one shop, when who should I see across the street coming out of the Mary Boone Gallery but Tobias and this really sleek-looking old woman. Well, not too old, but beaky, and she was wearing half the Canadian national output of furs. She'd make a better-looking man than a woman. You know, that sort of looks. And after looking at her a bit more, I realized from her looks that she had to be Tobias's mother, and the fact that they were arguing loaned credence to this theory. She reminds me of something Elvissa used to say, that if one member of a couple is too striking looking, then they should hope to have a boy rather than a girl because the girl will just end up looking like a curiosity rather than a beauty. So Tobias's parents had him instead. I can see where he got his looks. I bounced over to say hi."

"And?"

"I think Tobias was relieved to escape from their argument. He gave me a kiss that practically froze our lips together, it was that cold out, and then he swung me around to meet this woman, saying, 'Claire, this is my mother, E*lena*.' Imagine pronouncing your mother's name to someone like it was a joke. Such rudeness.

"Anyway, E*lena* was hardly the same woman who danced the samba carrying a pitcher of lemonade in Washington, D.C., long ago. She looked like she'd been heavily shrinkwrapped since then; I could sense a handful of pill vials chattering away in her handbag. The first thing she says to me is 'My, how *healthy* you look. So tanned.' Not even a hello. She had a civil enough manner, but I think she was using her talking-to-a-shop-clerk voice.

"When I told Tobias that the restaurant we were going to go to was closed, she offered to take us up to 'her restaurant' for lunch uptown. I thought that was sweet, but Tobias was hesitant, not that it mattered, since Elena overrode him. I don't think he ever lets his mother see the people in his life, and she was just curious.

"So off we went to Broadway, the two of them toasty warm in their furs (Tobias was wearing a fur – what a dink.) while me and my bones were clattering away in mere quilted cotton. Elena was telling me about her art collection ('I *live* for art') while we were toddling through this broken backdrop of carbonized buildings that smelled salty-fishy like caviar, grown men with ponytails wearing Kenzo, and mentally ill homeless people with AIDS being ignored by just about everybody."

"What restaurant did you go to?"

"We cabbed. I forget the name: up in the east sixties. *Trop chic*, though. Everything is *très trop chic* these days: lace and candles and dwarf forced narcissi and cut glass. It smelled lovely, like powdered sugar, and they simply *fawned* over Elena. We got a banquette booth, and the menus were written in chalk on an easeled board, the way I like because it makes the space so cozy. But what was curious was the way the waiter faced the menu board only toward me and Tobias. But when I went to move it, Tobias said, 'Don't bother. Elena's allergic to all known food groups. The only thing she eats here is seasoned millet and rainwater they bring down from Vermont in a zinc can.'

"I laughed at this but stopped really quickly when Elena made a face that told me this was, in fact, correct. Then the waiter came to tell her she had a phone call and she disappeared for the whole meal.

"Oh – for what it's worth, Tobias says hello," Claire says, lighting another cigarette.

"Gee. How thoughtful."

"Alright, alright. Sarcasm noted. It may be one in the morning here, but I'm not missing things *yet*. Where was I? Right – Tobias and I are alone for the first time. So do I ask him what's on my mind? About why he ditched me in Palm Springs or where our relationship is going? *Of course not*. I sat there and babbled and ate the food, which, I must say, was truly delicious: a celery root salad rémoulade and John Dory fish in Pernod sauce. *Yum*.

"The meal actually went quickly. Before I knew it, Elena returned and *zoom*: we're out of the restaurant, *zoom*: I got a peck-peck on the cheeks, and then *zoom*: she was in a cab off toward Lexington Avenue. No wonder Tobias is so rude. Look at his *training*.

"So we were out on the curb and there was a vacuum of activity. I think the last thing either of us wanted then was to talk. We drifted up Fifth Avenue to the Met, which was lovely and warm inside, all full of museum echoes and well-dressed children. But Tobias had to wreck whatever mood there may have been when he made this great big scene at the coat check stand, telling the poor woman there to put his coat out back so the animal rights activists couldn't splat it with a paint bomb. After that we slipped into the Egyptian statue area. God, those people were teeny weeny.

"Am I talking too long?"

"No. It's Armand's money, anyway."

"Okay. The *point* of all this is that finally, in front of the

Coptic pottery shards, with the two of us just feeling so futile pretending there was something between us when we both knew there was nothing, he decided to tell me what's on his mind – Andy, hang on a second. I'm starving. Let me go raid the fridge."

"Right now? This is the best part—" But Claire has plonked down the receiver. I take advantage of her disappearance to remove my travel-rumpled jacket and to pour a glass of water, allowing the water in the tap to run for fifteen seconds to displace the stale water in the pipes. I then turn on a lamp and sit comfortably in a sofa with my legs on the ottoman.

"I'm back," says Claire, "with some lovely cheesecake. Are you going to help Dag tend bar at Bunny Hollander's party tomorrow night?"

(What party?)

"What party?"

"I guess Dag hasn't told you yet."

"Claire, what did Tobias say?"

I hear her take in a breath. "He told me *part* of the truth, at least. He said he knew the only reason I liked him was for his looks and that there was no point in my denying it. (Not that I *tried*.) He said he knows that his looks are the only thing lovable about him and so that he might as well use them. Isn't that sad?"

I mumble agreement, but I think about what Dag had said last week, that Tobias had some other, questionable reason for seeing Claire – for crossing mountains when he could have had anyone. That, to me, is a more important confession. Claire reads my mind:

CONTROL IS NOT CONTROL

"But the using wasn't just one way. He said that my main attraction for him was his conviction that I knew a secret about life – some magic insight I had that gave me the strength to quit everyday existence. He said he was curious about the lives you, Dag, and I have built here on the fringe out in California. And he wanted to get my secret for himself – for an escape he hoped to make – except that he realized by listening to us talk that there was no way he'd ever really do it. He'd never have the guts to live up to complete freedom. The lack of rules would terrify him. *I don't know.* It sounded like unconvincing horseshit to me. It sounded a bit *too pat*, like he'd been coached. Would *you* believe it?"

Of course I wouldn't believe a word of it, but I abstain from giving an opinion. "I'll stay out of that. But at least it ended cleanly – no messy afterbirth . . ."

"*Cleanly?* Hey, as we were leaving the gallery and heading up Fifth Avenue, we even did the *let's-still-be-friends* thing. Talk about pain *free*. But it was when we were both walking and freezing and thinking of how we'd both gotten off the hook so easily that I found the stick.

"It was a Y-shaped tree branch that the parks people had dropped from a truck. Perfectly shaped like a water dowsing rod. Well! Talk about an object speaking to you from beyond! It just woke me up, and never in my life have I lunged so instinctively for an object as though it were intrinsically a part of me – like a leg or an arm I'd casually misplaced for twenty-seven years.

"I lurched forward, picked it up in my hands, rubbed it gently, getting bark scrapes on my black leather gloves, then grabbed onto both sides of the forks and rotated my hands inward – the classic water dowser's pose.

"Tobias said, 'What are you doing? Put that down, you're embarrassing me,' just as you'd expect, but I held right on to it, all the way down Fifth to Elena's in the fifties, where we were going for coffee.

"Elena's turned out to be this huge thirties Moderne co-op, white *ev*erything, with pop explosion paintings, evil little lap dogs, and a maid scratching lottery tickets in the kitchen. The whole trip. His family sure has extreme taste.

"But I could tell as we were coming through the door that the rich food from lunch and the late night before were catching up with me. Tobias went to make a phone call in a back room while I took my jacket and shoes off and lay down on a couch to veg-out and watch the sun fade behind the Lipstick Building. It was like instant annihilation – that instant fuzzy bumble-bee anxiety-free afternoony exhaustion that you never get at night. Before I could even *analyze* it, I turned into furniture.

"I must have been asleep for hours. When I woke it was dark out and the temperature had gone down. There was an Arapaho blanket on top of me and the glass table was covered with junk that wasn't there before: potato chip bags, magazines. . . . But none of it made any sense to me. You know how sometimes after an afternoon nap you wake up with the shakes or anxiety? That's what happened to me. I couldn't remember who I was or where I was or what time of year it was or *anything*. All I knew was that I *was*. I felt so wide open, so vulnerable, like a great big field that's just been harvested. So when Tobias came out from the kitchen, saying, 'Hello, Rumpelstiltskin,' I had a flash of remembrance and I was so relieved that I started to bellow. Tobias came over to me and said, 'Hey, what's the matter? Don't cry on the fabric . . . come here, baby.' But I just grabbed his arm and hyperventilated. I think it confused him.

"After a minute of this, I calmed down, blew my nose on a paper towel that was lying on the coffee table, and then reached for my dowsing branch and held it to my chest. Tobias said, 'Oh, God, you're not going to fixate on the *twig* again, are you? Look, I *really* didn't realize a breakup would affect you so much. Sorry.'

"'Excuse me?' I say. 'I can quite deal with our breakup, thank you. Don't flatter yourself. I'm thinking of *other* things.'

"'Like what?'

"'Like I finally know for sure who I'm going to fall in love with. The news came to me while I was sleeping.'

"'*Share* it with me, Claire.'

"'Possibly you'll understand this, Tobias. When I get back to California, I'm going to take this stick and head out in the desert. I'm going to spend every second of my free time out there – dowsing for water buried deep. I'm going to bake in the heat and walk for miles and miles across the nothingness – maybe see a roadrunner and maybe get bitten by a rattler or a sidewinder. And one day, I don't know when, I'm going to come over a sand dune and I'll find someone else out there dowsing for water, too. And I don't know who that someone will be, but *that's* who I'm going to fall in love with. Someone who's dowsing for water, just like me.'

"I reached for a bag of potato chips on the table. Tobias says to me, 'That's really *great*, Claire. Be sure you wear hot pants and no panties and maybe you can hitchhike and you can have biker-sex in vans with strange men.'

"But I ignored his comment, and then, as I was reaching for a potato chip there on the glass table, I found behind the bag a bottle of Honolulu Choo-Choo nail polish.

"*Well*.

"Tobias saw me pick it up and stare at the label. He smiled as my mind went blank and then was replaced by this horrible feeling – like something from one of Dag's horror stories where a character is driving along in a Chrysler K-Car and then the character suddenly realizes there's a murderous drifter hidden behind the bench seat holding a piece of rope.

"I grabbed for my shoes and started to put them on. Then my jacket. I curtly said it was time I got going. That's when Tobias started lashing into me with this slow growly voice.

YOU
MIGHT NOT
COUNT
IN THE
NEW ORDER

'You're just so sublime, aren't you, Claire. Looking for your delicate little insights with your hothouse freak show buddies out in Hell-with-Palm-Trees, aren't you? Well I'll tell you something, I like my job here in the city. I like the hours and the mind games and the battling for money and status tokens, even though you think I'm sick for wanting any part of it.'

"But I was already heading for the door; passing by the kitchen I saw briefly, but clearly enough, two milk-white crossed legs and a puff of cigarette smoke, all cropped by a door frame. Tobias was close on my heels as he followed me out into the hallway and toward the elevators. He kept going, he said, 'You know, when I first met you, Claire, I thought that here might finally be a chance for me to be a class-act for once. To develop something sublime about myself. Well fuck sublime, Claire. I don't want dainty little moments of insight. I want everything and I want it now. I want to be ice-picked on the head by a herd of angry cheerleaders, Claire. Angry cheerleaders on drugs. You don't get that, do you?'

"I had pushed the elevator button and was staring at the doors, which couldn't seem to open soon enough. He kicked away one of the dogs that had followed us, continuing his tirade.

"'I want action. I want to be radiator steam hissing on the cement of the Santa Monica freeway after a thousand-car pile up – with acid rock from the smashed cars roaring in the background. I want to be the man in the black hood who switches on the air raid sirens. I want to be naked and windburned and riding the lead missile of a herd heading over to bomb every little fucking village in New Zealand.'

"Fortunately, the door finally opened. I got inside and looked at Tobias without saying anything. He was still aiming and firing: 'Just go to hell, Claire. You and your superior attitude. We're all lapdogs; I just happen to know who's petting me. But hey – if more people like you choose not to play the game, it's easier for people like me to win.'

"The door closed and I just waved good-bye, and when I began descending, I was shaking a bit – but the backseat drifter was gone. I was released from the obsession, and before I'd reached the lobby I couldn't believe what a brain-dead glutton I'd been – for sex, for humiliation, for pseudodrama. . . . And I planned right there never to repeat this sort of experience ever again. The only way you can deal with the Tobiases of this world is to not let them into your lives *at all*. Blind yourself to their wares. God, I felt re*lieved*; not the least bit angry."

We both consider her words.

"Eat some of your cheesecake, Claire. I need time to digest all this."

"Naah. I can't eat; I've lost my appetite. What a day. Oh, by the way, could you do a favor for me? Could you put some flowers in a vase for me in my place for when I get back tomorrow? Some tulips, maybe? I'm going to need them."

"Oh. Does this mean you'll be back living in your old bungalow again?"

"Yes."

PLASTICS
NEVER
DISINTEGRATE

Today is a day of profound meteorologic interest. Dust tornadoes have struck the hills of Thunderbird Cove down the
valley where the Fords live; all desert cities are on a flash-flood
alert. In Rancho Mirage, an oleander hedge has made a poor
sieve and has allowed a prickly mist of tumbleweed, palm
skirting, and desiccated empty tubs of Big Gulp slush drink to
pelt the wall of the Barbara Sinatra Children's Center. Yet the
air is warm and the sun contradictorily shines. ¶"Welcome
back, Andy," calls Dag. "This is what weather was like back in
the sixties." He's waist deep in the swimming pool, skimming
the water's surface with a net. "Just *look* at the big big sky up
there. And guess what – while you were away the landlord
cheaped-out and bought a secondhand cover sheet for the
pool. Look at what happened—" ¶What *happened*, was that
the sheet of bubble-wrap covering, after years of sunlight and
dissolved granulated swimming pool chlorine, has reached a
critical point; the covering's resins have begun to disintegrate,
releasing into the water thousands of delicate, fluttery plastic
petal blossoms that had previously encased air bubbles. The
curious dogs, their golden paws going *clack-clack* on the pool's

cement edge, peek into the water, sniffing but not drinking, and they briefly inspect Dag's legs, which, with the small dots of rotting plastic fluttering about, remind me of an April Tuesday in Tokyo, of cherry blossoms falling to the earth. Dag tells them to scram, that there's nothing edible here.

"Thanks, but no. I'll let you have all the fun to yourself. Did Claire tell you her news?"

"About good riddance to Slime-O? She called this morning. I must say I admire that girl's romantic spirit."

"Yes, she's a *treat*, alright."

"She gets back tonight around eleven. And we have a surprise all planned for you tomorrow, too. We think you'll like it. You weren't going anywhere tomorrow, were you?"

"No."

"Good."

We discuss the holidays and their general lack of amusement value, all the while with Dag skimming away. I haven't yet asked any questions about the Skipper or the Aston Martin mess.

"You know, I always thought that plastics never decompose, but they *do*. Just *look* – this is so great. And guess what – I've also devised a way to get rid of all the world's plutonium – safely and forever. I've been just *so* clever while everyone was away."

"I'm glad to hear you've solved the biggest problem of our time, Dag. Why do I get the feeling you're going to tell me?"

"How perceptive of you. It works like this—" Wind ripples a cluster of petals directly into Dag's net. "You take all of the plutonium that's lying around, you know, the big chunks that they use as doorstops at power plants. You take these big doorstop chunks and coat them in steel, just like M & M

Dumpster Clocking: The tendency when looking at objects to guesstimate the amount of time they will take to eventually decompose: *"Ski boots are the worst. Solid plastic. They'll be around till the sun goes super nova."*

candies, and then you put them in a rocket and fire them out over land. That way, if the rocket crashes, you just go and pick up the M & Ms and try again. But the rockets *won't* crash, and the plutonium gets fired *right into the sun*."

"That sounds okay, Dag, but what if the rocket crashes in water and the plutonium sinks?"

"You fire it toward the North Pole, so it lands on ice. And if it *does* sink, you send out a submarine to pick it up. It's idiot-proof. Gosh, I'm clever."

"You're sure no one's thought of this already?"

"Maybe. But it's still the best idea going. By the way, you're helping me tend bar tonight at the big party at Bunny Hollander's. I put you on the list. It'll be fun. That's assuming, of course, that the winds today don't blow all of our houses to bits. Jesus, *listen* to them."

"So, Dag, what about the Skipper?"

"What about him?"

"Think he'll narc on you?"

"If he does, I'll deny it. You'll deny it, too. Two versus one. I'm not into being prosecuted for felonies."

The thought of anything legal or prison oriented petrifies me. Dag can read this on my face: "Don't sweat it, sport. It'll never come to that. I promise. And guess what. You won't believe whose car it was . . ."

"Whose?"

"Bunny Hollander's. The guy whose party we're catering tonight."

"Oh, Lord."

Fickle dove-gray klieg light spots twitch and dart underneath tonight's overcast clouds, like the recently released contents of Pandora's box.

I'm in Las Palmas, behind the elaborate wet bar of Bunny Hollander's sequin-enhanced New Year's gala. *Nouveaux riches*

The Tens: The first decade of a new century.

faces are pushing themselves into mine, simultaneously bullying me for drinks (parvenu wealth always treats the help like dirt) and seeking my approval – and possibly my sexual favor.

It's a B-list crowd: TV money versus film money; too much attention given to bodies too late in life. Better-looking but a bit too flash; the deceiving pseudohealth of sunburned fat people; the facial anonymity found only among babies, the elderly, and the overly face-lifted. There is a hint of celebrities, but none are actually present; too much money and not enough famous people can be a deadly mix. And while the party most definitely roars, the lack of famed mortals vexes the host, Bunny Hollander.

Bunny is a local celebrity. He produced a hit Broadway show in 1956, *Kiss Me, Mirror* or some such nonsense, and has been coasting on it for almost thirty-five years. He has glossy gray hair, like a newspaper left out in the rain, and a permanent leer that makes him resemble a child molester, the result of chain face-lifts since the nineteen sixties. But then Bunny knows lots of disgusting jokes and he treats staff well – the best combo going – so that makes up for his defects.

Dag opens a bottle of white: "Bunny looks like he's got dismembered Cub Scouts buried under his front porch."

"We've *all* got dismembered Cub Scouts under our front porches, Honey," says Bunny, slinking (in spite of his corpulence) up from behind and passing Dag his glass. "Ice for the drinky-winky, please." He winks, wags his bum, and leaves.

For once, Dag blushes. "I don't think I've ever seen a human being with so many secrets. Too bad about his car. Wish it was someone I didn't like."

Later on I obliquely raise the subject of the burned car to Bunny, trying to answer a question in my mind: "Saw your car

---

Metaphasia: An inability to perceive metaphor.

Dorian Graying: The unwillingness to gracefully allow one's body to show signs of aging.

in the paper, Bunny. Didn't it used to have an *Ask Me About My Grandchildren* bumper sticker?"

"Oh *that*. A little prank from my Vegas buddies. Charming lads. We don't talk about *them*." Discussion closed.

The Hollander estate was built in the era of the first moon launches and resembles the fantasy lair of an extremely vain and terribly wicked international jewel thief of that era. Platforms and mirrors abound. There are Noguchi sculptures and Calder mobiles; the wrought-iron work is all of an atomic orbital motif. The bar, covered in teak, might well be identical to one in, say, a successful London advertising agency in the era of Twiggy. The lighting and architecture are designed primarily to make everyone look *fa*-bulous.

In spite of the celebrity shortage, the party is *fa*-bulous, as just about everybody keeps reminding each other. Social creature that Bunny is, he knows what makes a joint hop. "A party is simply *not* a party without bikers, transvestites, and fashion models," he sings from beside the chafing dishes loaded with skinless duck in Chilean blueberry sauce.

He says this, of course, fully confident that all of these types (and more) are present. Only the disenfranchised can party with abandon – the young, the genuinely rich elderly, the freakishly beautiful, the kinked, the outlawed. . . . Hence, the soiree is pleasingly devoid of yuppies, an observation I pass on to Bunny on his nineteenth round of vodka tonics. "You might as well invite *trees* to a party as invite yupplings, Dear," he says. "Oh, look – there's the hot air balloon!" He disappears.

Dag is in his element tonight, with bartending a mere aside to his own personal agenda of cocktail consumption (he has lousy bartender's ethics) and intense chats and fevered arguments with guests. Most of the time he's not even at the bar and is off roaming the house and the starkly lit cactus garden grounds, coming back only intermittently with reports.

"Andy – I just had the *best* time. I was helping the Filipino guy toss deboned chicken carcasses to the rottweilers. They've been caged for the evening. And that Swedish lady with the bionic-looking nylon leg splint was getting it all on 16mm. Says she fell into an excavation site in Lesotho that almost turned her legs into *osso buco*."

"That's great, Dag. Now could you pass me two bottles of red please."

"Sure." He passes me the wine, then lights up a cigarette – not even the most cursory gesture toward tending bar. "I was talking to that Van Klijk lady, too – the super-old one with the muumuu and the fox pelts who owns half the newspapers in the west. She told me that her brother Cliff seduced her in Monterey at the beginning of World War II, and then somehow got himself drowned in a submarine off of Helgoland. Ever since then she can only live in a hot, dry climate – the opposite of doomed and crippled submarines. But the way she told the story, I think she tells it to *everyone*."

How does Dag extract these things from strangers?

Way over by the main entrance, where some seventeen-year-old girls from the Valley with detexturized mermaid hair are frugging with a record producer, I see some police officers enter. Such is the party that I'm not sure if they're simply more "types" carted in by Bunny to boost the atmosphere. Bunny is talking and laughing with the officers, none of whom Dag sees. Bunny toddles over.

"*Herr Bellinghausen* – If I'd known you were a desperate criminal, I would have given you an invi*tation* instead of employment. The forces of respectability are asking for you at the door. I don't know what they want, Dear, but if you make a scene, do a favor and be *visual*."

Bunny again flits off, and Dag's face blanches. He grimaces

Obscurism: The practice of peppering daily life with obscure references (forgotten films, dead TV stars, unpopular books, defunct countries, etc.) as a subliminal means of showcasing both one's education and one's wish to disassociate from the world of mass culture.

at me and then walks through an open set of glass doors, away from the police, and down toward the end of the yard.

"Pietro," I say, "can you cover for me a moment? I have to go do something. Ten minutes."

"Bring me a sample," says Pietro, assuming that I'm off to the parking lot to check out the substance scene. But, of course, I go to follow Dag.

"I've been wondering what this moment would feel like for a long time," says Dag – "this moment of finally getting caught. I actually feel relieved. Like I've just quit a job. Did I ever tell you the story about the guy from the suburbs who was terrified of getting VD?" Dag is drunk enough to be revealing, but not drunk enough to be stupid. His legs are dangling off the end of a cement flash-flood pipe in the wash next to Bunny's house where I find him.

"Ten years he spent pestering his doctor for blood samples and Wassermann tests, until finally (after doing *what* I'm not sure) he actually *did* end up getting a dose. So then he says to his doctor, 'Oh – well I'd better get some penicillin then.' He took his treatment and he never thought about the disease ever again. He just wanted to get caught. That's all."

I can't conceive of a less wise place to be sitting at the moment. Flash floods really are *flash* floods. One moment everything's hunkydory, the next there's this foaming white broth of sagebrush, abandoned sofas, and drowned coyotes.

Standing below the pipe, I can only see his legs. Such are the acoustics that his voice is resonating and baritone. I climb up and sit next to him. There's moonlight but no moon visible and a single point of light comes from the tip of his cigarette. He throws a rock out into the dark.

"You'd better go back up to the party, Dag. I mean, before the cops start pistol-whipping Bunny's guests, making them reveal your hiding spot, or something."

"Soon enough. Give me a moment – looks like the days of Dag the Vandal are over, Andy. Cigarette?"

"Not right now."

"Tell you what. I'm a little bit freaked out at the moment. Why don't you tell me a short story – anything will do – and then I'll go up."

"Dag, this really isn't the time . . ."

"Just *one* story, Andy, and yes, it *is* the time."

I'm on the spot, but curiously, a small story comes to mind. "Fair enough. Here goes. When I was in Japan years ago – on a student exchange program – I was once living with this family and they had a daughter, maybe four years old. Cute little thing.

"So anyway, after I moved in (I was there for maybe a half year), she refused to acknowledge my presence within the household. Things I said to her at the dinner table were ignored. She'd walk right by me in the hall. I mean I did not exist *at all* in her universe. This was, of course, very insulting; everyone likes to think of themselves as the sort of charmed human being whom animals and small children instinctively adore.

"The situation was also annoying, but then there was nothing really to be done about it; no efforts on my part could get her to say my name or respond to my presence.

"So then one day I came home to find that papers in my room had been cut up into bits – letters and drawings I had been working on for some time – cut and drawn on with obvious small child malicious finesse. I was furious. And as she sauntered by my room shortly thereafter, I couldn't help myself and began to scold her rather loudly for what she had done, in both English and Japanese.

THE SUN IS NOT YOUR ENEMY

"Of course, I felt bad right away. She walked away and I wondered if I had gone too far. But a few minutes later she brought me her pet beetle in its little cage (a popular Asian children's amusement), grabbed me by the arm, and led me out into the garden. There, she began to tell stories of her insect's secret life. The point was that she had to get punished for something before she could open communication. She must be twelve years old now. I got a postcard from her about a month ago."

I don't think Dag was listening. He should have been. But he just wanted to hear a voice. We throw more rocks. Then, out of the blue, Dag asks me if I know how I'm going to die.

"Bellinghausen, don't get morbid on me, okay. Just go up there and deal with the police. They've probably only got questions. That's all."

"*Fermez la bouche*, Andy. It was rhetorical. Let me tell you how I think *I'm* going to die. It's like this. I'll be seventy and be sitting out here in the desert, no dentures – all of my own teeth – wearing gray tweed. I'll be planting flowers – thin, fragile flowers that are lost causes in a desert – like those little cartoon flowers that clowns wear on top of their heads – in little clown's hat pots. There'll be no sound save for the hum of heat, and my body will cast no shadow, hunched over with a spade clinking against the stony soil. The sun will be right overhead and behind me there'll be this terrific flapping of wings – louder than the flapping any bird can make.

"Turning slowly around, I will almost be blinded as I see that an angel has landed, gold and unclothed, taller than me by a head. I will put down the small flowerpot I'm holding – somehow it seems sort of embarrassing. And I will take one more breath, my last.

"From there, the angel will reach under my flimsy bones and take me into its arms, and from there it is only a matter of time before I am carried, soundlessly and with absolute affection, directly into the sun."

Dag tosses his cigarette and refocuses his hearing to the sounds of the party, faint over the gully. "Well, Andy. Wish me luck," he says, hopping down off of the cement pipe, then taking a few steps, stopping, turning around then saying to me, "Here, bend over to me a second." I comply, whereupon he kisses me, triggering films in my mind of liquefied supermarket ceilings cascading upward toward heaven. "There. I've always wanted to do that."

He returns to the big shiny party.

A W A I T
L I G H T N I N G

New Year's Day. ¶I can already smell the methane of Mexico, a stone's throw away, while I bake in a Calexico, California traffic jam, waiting to cross the border while embroiled in wavering emphysemic mirages of diesel spew. My car rests on a braiding and decomposing six-lane corridor lit by a tired winter sunset. Inching along with me in this linear space is a true gift-sampler of humanity and its vehicles: three-abreast tattooed farm workers in pickup trucks, enthusiastically showcasing a variety of country and western tunes; mirror-windowed sedan loads of chilled and Ray-Banned yuppies (a faint misting of Handel and Philip Glass); local *hausfraus* in hair curlers, off to get cheaper Mexicali groceries while inhaling *Soap Opera Digest* within cheerfully stickered Hyundais; retired look-alike Canadian couples bickering over maps falling apart from having been folded and unfolded so many times. To the side, peso brokers with Japanese names inhabit booths painted the bright colors of sugar candies. I hear dogs. And if I want a spurious fast food hamburger or Mexican car insurance papers, any number of nearby merchants will all too easily cater to this whim. Under the hood of the Volkswagen are two dozen bottles of Evian water and a flask of Immodium antidiarrheal – certain bourgeois habits die hard.

Last night I got in at five, exhausted from closing down the bar myself. Pietro and the other bartender split early to go trolling for babes at the Pompeii night club; Dag left with the police to go do something down at the station. When I got home, all of the lights were out in the bungalows and I went right to bed – news of Dag's brush with the law and a welcome home for Claire would have to wait.

What I found when I got up the next morning around eleven was a note taped to my front door. Claire's handwriting:

hunny bunny,

we're off to san felipe! mexico beckons. dag and I talked over the holidays and he convinced me that now's the time, so we're going to buy a little hotel . . . why not join us? I mean, what else were we going to do? and imagine, us hoteliers? the brain boggles.

we've kidnapped the doggies but we'll let you come of your own free will. it gets cold at night so bring blankies. and books. and pencils. the town is supertiny, so to find us just look for dag's wagoon. we're waiting for you très impatiently. expect to see you tonight

luv,
claire

At the bottom Dag had written:

CLEAN OUT YOUR SAVINGS ACCOUNT, PALMER.
GET DOWN HERE. WE NEED YOU.
P.S.: CHECK YOUR ANSWERING MACHINE

On the answer machine I found the following message:

"Greetings Palmer. See you got the note. Excuse my speech, but I'm totally fried. Got in last night at four and I haven't bothered to sleep – I can do that in the car on the way to Mexico. I told you we had a surprise for you. Claire said, and she's right, that if we let you think about the hotel idea too much, you'd never come. You analyze things too much. So don't think about this – just come, okay? We'll talk about it when you get here.

"As for the law, guess what? The Skipper got brained by a GTO driven by global teens from Orange County yesterday, just outside the Liquor Barn. Quelle good fortune! In his pockets they found all of these demented letters written to me telling about how he was going to make me burn just like that car, and so forth. Moi! I mean, talk about terror. So I told the police (not untruly, I might add) that I'd seen the Skipper at the scene of the crime and I figured the Skipper was worried that I might report him. Talk about neat. So it's case closed, but I think this little funster's had enough vandalism for nine lives.

"Anyhow, we'll see you in San Felipe. Drive safely (God, what a geriatric comment to make) and we'll see you toni . . ."

"Hey, dickface, move your butt!" hectors the short-fused Romeo to the rear, tailgating me in his chartreuse rust-bucket flatbed.

Back to real life. Time to get snappy. Time to get a life. But it's hard.

Disengaging the clutch, I lurch forward, one car's length closer to the border – one unit closer to a newer, less-monied

---

Terminal Wanderlust: A condition common to people of transient middle-class upbringings. Unable to feel rooted in any one environment, they move continually in the hopes of finding an idealized sense of community in the next location.

world, where a different food chain carves its host landscape in alien ways I can scarcely comprehend. Once I cross that border, for example, automobile models will mysteriously end around the decidedly Texlahoman year of 1974, the year after which engine technologies became overcomplex and non-tinkerable – *uncannibalizable*. I will find a landscape punctuated by oxidized, spray painted and shot-at "half-cars" – demi-wagons cut lengthwise, widthwise, and heightwise, stripped of parts and culturally invisible, like the black-hooded Bunraku puppet masters of Japan.

Further along, in San Felipe where my – *our* – hotel may some day exist, I will find fences built of whalebones, chromed Toyota bumpers, and cactus spines woven into barbed wire. And down the town's deliriously white beaches there will be spare figures of street urchins, their faces obscured and over-exposed by the brightness of the sun, hopelessly vending cakey ropes of false pearls and lobular chains of fool's gold.

This will be my new landscape.

From my driver's seat in Calexico I see sweating mobs ahead of me, crossing the border on foot, toting straw bags chockablock with anticancer drugs, tequila, two-dollar violins, and Corn Flakes.

Cryptotechnophobia: The secret belief that technology is more of a menace than a boon.

Virgin Runway: A travel destination chosen in the hopes that no one else has chosen it.

Native Aping: Pretending to be a native when visiting a foreign destination.

Expatriate Solipsism: When arriving in a foreign travel destination one had hoped was undiscovered, only to find many people just like oneself; the peeved refusal to talk to said people because they have ruined one's elitist travel fantasy.

And I see the fence on the border, the chain-link border fence that reminds me of certain photos of Australia – photos in which anti-rabbit fencing has cleaved the landscape in two: one side of the fence nutritious, food secreting, and bursting with green; the other side lunar, granular, parched, and desperate. I think of Dag and Claire when I think of this split – and the way they chose by free will to inhabit that lunar side of the fence – enacting their difficult destinies: Dag doomed forever to gaze longingly at his sun; Claire forever traversing her sands with her dowsing rod, praying to find water below. And me . . .

Yes, well, what *about* me?

I'm on the lunar side of the fence, that much I know for sure. I don't know where or how, but I definitely made that choice. And lonely and awful as that choice can sometimes be, I have no regrets.

And I do *two* things on my side of the fence, and both of these things are the occupations of characters in two *very* short stories I'll quickly tell.

The *first* story was actually a failure when I told it to Dag and Claire a few months ago: "The Young Man Who Desperately Wanted to Be Hit by Lightning."

As the title may indicate, it is the tale of a young man who worked at a desperately boring job for an unthinking corporation who one day gave up everything – a young fiancée flushed and angry at the altar, his career advancement prospects, and everything else he had ever worked for – all to travel across the prairies in a beat-up old Pontiac in pursuit of storms, despondent that he might go through his entire life without being struck by lightning.

I say the story was a failure, because, well, *nothing happened*. At the end of the telling, Young Man was still out there somewhere in Nebraska or Kansas, running around holding a shower curtain rod up to the heavens, praying for a miracle.

Emallgration: Migration toward lower-tech, lower-information environments containing a lessened emphasis on consumerism.

Dag and Claire went nuts with curiosity, wanting to know where Young Man ended up, but his fate remains a cliff-hanger; I sleep better at night knowing that Young Man roams the badlands.

The second story, well, it's a bit more complex, and I've never told anyone before. It's about a young man – *oh, get real* – it's about *me*.

It's about *me* and something else I want desperately to have happen to *me*, more than just about anything.

This is what I want: I want to lie on the razory brain-shaped rocks of Baja. I want to lie on these rocks with no plants around me, traces of brine on my fingers and a chemical sun burning up in the heaven. There will be no sound, perfect silence, just me and oxygen, not a thought in my mind, with pelicans diving into the ocean beside me for glimmering mercury bullets of fish.

Small cuts from the rocks will extract blood that will dry as quickly as it flows, and my brain will turn into a thin white cord stretched skyward up into the ozone layer and humming like a guitar string. And like Dag on the day of his death, I will hear wings, too, except the wings I hear will be from a pelican, flying in from the ocean – a great big dopey, happy-looking pelican that will land at my side and then, with smooth leathery feet, waddle over to my face, without fear and with an elegant flourish – showing the grace of a thousand wine stewards – offer before me the gift of a small silvery fish.

I would sacrifice *any*thing to be given this offering.

JAN. 01, 2000

I drove to Calexico this afternoon by way of the Salton Sea, a
huge saline lake and the lowest elevation in the U.S. I drove
through the Box Canyon, through El Centro . . . Calipatria . . .
Brawley . . . . ¶There is a sense of great pride in the land here
in Imperial County – "*America's Winter Garden.*" After the
harsh barrenness of the desert, this region's startling fecun-
dity – its numberless fields of sheep and spinach and
dalmation-skinned cows – feels biologically surreal. *Everything*
secretes food here. Even the Laotian-looking date palms that
colonnade the highway. ¶Roughly an hour ago, while driving
to the border within this landscape of overwhelming fertility,
an unusual incident happened to me – an incident I feel I
must talk about. It went like this: ¶I had just driven into the
Salton basin from the north, via the Box Canyon road. I
entered the region in a good mood at the lemon groves of a
small citrus town called Mecca. I'd just stolen a warm orange
the size of a bowling ball from a roadside grove and a farmer
rounding a corner on a tractor had caught me; all he did was
smile, reach into a bag beside him and throw me another. A
farmer's forgiveness felt very absolute. ¶Back in my car I'd

closed the windows and was peeling the orange to trap the smell inside, and I was driving and getting sticky juice all over the steering wheel, wiping my hands off on my pants. But driving over a hill I was suddenly able to see the horizon for the first time that day – over the Salton Sea – and there I saw a sight that made my heart almost hop out of my mouth, a sight that made my feet reflexively hit the brakes.

It was a vision that could only have come from one of Dag's bedtime stories: it was a thermonuclear cloud – as high in the sky as the horizon is far away – angry and thick, with an anvil-shaped head the size of a medieval kingdom and as black as a bedroom at night.

My orange fell to the floor. I pulled the car to the roadside, serenaded as I did so by a rusted honking El Camino full of migrant workers that almost rear ended me. But there was no doubting it: *yes*, the cloud was on the horizon. It was not imaginary. It was that same cloud I'd been dreaming of steadily since I was five, shameless, exhausted, and gloating.

I panicked; blood rushed to my ears; I waited for the sirens; I turned on the radio. The biopsy had come back positive. Could a *critical situation* have occurred since the noon news? Surprisingly there was nothing on the airwaves – just more ice rink music and a few trickling Mexican radio stations. Had I gone mad? Why was nobody reacting? Cars casually passed me coming the other way, no hint of urgency in their demeanors. And so I was left with no choice; possessed with lurid curiosity, I drove on.

The cloud was so enormous that it defied perspective. I realized this as I was approaching Brawley, a small town fifteen miles from the border. Every time I thought I'd reached the cloud's ground zero, I would realize that the cloud's locus was still far away. Finally I got so close that its rubber-black stem occupied the whole front of my windshield. *Mountains* never seemed this big, but then mountains, in spite of their ambitions, can never annex the atmosphere. And to think that Dag told me these clouds were *small*.

At last, at the Highway 86 junction where I turned sharply

right, I was able to see the roots of this mushroom. Its simple source both made instant sense and filled me with profound relief: farmers within a small area were burning off the stubble of their fields. The stratospheric black monster created by the frail orange rope of flame that ran across their fields was insanely out of proportion to the deed – this smoke cloud visible for five hundred miles – *visible from outer space*.

The event had also become something of a chance tourist attraction. Traffic had slowed down to a trickle past the burning fields, and scores of vehicles had stopped, including mine. The *pièce de résistance*, aside from the smoke and flames, was what those flames left in their wake – recently charred fields now in lee of the wind.

These fields were carbonized to an absolute matte black of a hue that seemed more stellar in origin than anything on this planet. It was a supergravitational blackness unwilling to begrudge to spectators a single photon; black snow that defied XYZ perspective and that rested in front of the viewer's eye like a cut-out paper trapezoid. This blackness was so large, intense and blemishless that fighting, cranky children stopped squabbling inside their parents' mobile homes to stare. So did traveling salesmen in their beige sedans, stretching their legs and eating hamburgers microwaved back at the 7-Eleven.

Around me were Nissans and F-250s and Daihatsus and school buses. Most occupants leaned against their cars with arms crossed over their chests, silently respectful of the accidental wonder before them – a hot, dry silk black sheet, this marvel of antipurity. It was a restful unifying experience – like watching tornadoes off in the distance. It made us smile at each other.

Then, directly beside me I heard an engine noise. It was a van pulling over – a flashy-looking red candy-flake high-tech number with smoked windows – and out of it emerged, much to my surprise, a dozen or so mentally retarded young teenagers, male and female, gregarious and noisy, in high spirits and good moods with an assortment of flailing limbs and happy shouts of "hello!" to me.

Their driver was an exasperated-looking man of maybe forty, with a red beard and what appeared to be much experience as a chaperone. He herded his wards with a kind but rigid discipline, as might a mother goose tending her goslings, forcefully but with obvious kindness, grabbing them by the neck, offering them redirection.

The driver took his charges to a wooden fence that bordered the field and separated us and our cars from it. Then, amazingly after only a minute or so, the garrulous teens became silent.

It took me a second to realize what had silenced them. A cocaine white egret, a bird I had never seen in real life before, had flown in from the west, its reptilian instincts alert to the delicious offerings the burned fields would soon be bringing forth – now that so many new and wonderful tropisms had been activated by fire.

The bird was circling the field, and it seemed to me to belong more to the Ganges or the Nile rather than to America. And its jet-white contrast with the carbonized field was so astounding, so extreme, as to elicit gasps audible to me from most all of my neighbors, even those parked quite far down the road.

Then the reactions of my giggly, bouncy teenage neighbors became charmed and unified, as though they were watching a fireworks volley. They were *oohing* and *aahing* as the bird and its impossibly long hairy neck simply *refused* to land, circling and circling, affecting arcs and breathtaking swoops. Their enthusiasm was contagious, and I found myself, much to their great pleasure, *oohing* and *aahing* along, too.

And then the bird circled in retreat, westward, just down the road from us. We thought its culinary meditations were over, and there were mild *boos*. Then suddenly, the egret altered its arc. We quickly and excitedly realized that it was going to swoop right over *us*. We felt chosen.

One of the teens squealed alarmingly with delight. This caused me to look over in their direction. At that very moment, time must have accelerated slightly. Suddenly the children were turning to look at *me*, and I felt something sharp drag across my head, there was a *swoop swoop swoop* sound. The egret had grazed my head – it claw had ripped my scalp. I fell to my knees, but I didn't remove my eyes from the bird's progress.

All of us, in fact, turned our heads in unison and continued to watch our white visitor land in the field, occupying a position of absolute privilege. We watched, entranced, as it began to tug small creatures from the soil, and such was the moment's beauty that I essentially forgot I had been cut. Only when I idly reached up to brush fingers over my scalp to bring down a drop of blood on my finger did I realize the directness of the bird's contact.

I stood up and was considering this drop of blood when a pair of small fat arms grabbed around my waist, fat arms bearing fat dirty hands tipped with cracked fingernails. It was one of the mentally retarded teenagers, a girl in a sky blue calico dress, trying to pull my head down to her level. I could see her long, streaky, fine blond hair from my height, and she was drooling somewhat as she said, *urrd*, meaning bird, several times.

I bowed down on my knees again before her while she inspected my talon cut, hitting it gently with an optimistic and healing staccato caress – it was the faith-healing gesture of a child consoling a doll that has been dropped.

Then, from behind me I felt another pair of hands as one of her friends joined in. Then another pair. Suddenly I was dog-piled by an instant family, in their adoring, healing, uncritical embrace, each member wanting to show their affection more than the other. They began to hug me – too hard – as though I *were* a doll, unaware of the strength they exerted. I was being winded – crushed – pinched and trampled.

The man with the beard came over to yank them away. But how could I explain to him, this well-intentioned gentleman, that this discomfort, no this *pain*, I was experiencing was no problem at all, that, in fact, this crush of love was unlike anything I had ever known.

Well, maybe he *did* understand. He removed his hands from his wards as though they were giving him small static shocks, allowing them to continue crushing me with their warm assault of embraces. The man then pretended to watch the white bird feeding in the black field.

I can't remember whether I said thank you.

NUMBERS

Percent of U.S. budget spent on the elderly: 30
                          on education: 2
ROLLING STONE, APRIL 19, 1990, P. 43.

Number of dead lakes in Canada: 14,000
SOUTHAM NEWS SERVICES, OCTOBER 7, 1989.

Number of people in the workforce per Social Security bene-
ficiary . . .
     in 1949: 13
     in 1990: 3.4
     in 2030: 1.9

FORBES, NOVEMBER 14, 1988, P. 225.

Percentage of men aged 25–29 never married . . .
     in 1970: 19
     in 1987: 42
Percentage of women aged 25–29 never married . . .
     in 1970: 11
     in 1987: 29
AMERICAN DEMOGRAPHICS, NOVEMBER 1988.

Percentage of women aged 20–24 married . . .
     in 1960: 72
     in 1984: 43

Percentage of households under age 25 living in poverty . . .
    in 1979: 20
    in 1984: 33

U.S BUREAU OF THE CENSUS.

Number of human deaths possible from one pound of plutonium if finely ground up and inhaled: 42,000,000,000
1984 U.S. plutonium inventory, in pounds: 380,000
These numbers multiplied together: 16,000,000,000,000,000

SCIENCE DIGEST, JULY 1984.

Percentage of income required for a down payment on a first
home . . .
    in 1967: 22
    in 1987: 32
Percentage of 25–29 year olds owning homes . . .
    in 1973: 43.6
    in 1987: 35.9

FORBES, NOVEMBER 14, 1988.

Real change in cost of a one-carat diamond ring set in 18-
karat gold between 1957 and 1987:
    (in percent): +322
    of an eight-piece dining-room suite: +259
    of a movie admission: +180
    of an air flight to London, England: –80

REPORT ON BUSINESS, MAY 1988.

Chances that an American has been on TV: 1 in 4
Percentage of Americans who say they do not watch TV: 8
Number of hours per week spent watching TV by those who
say they do not watch TV: 10
Number of murders the average child has seen on television by
the age of sixteen: 18,000
Number of commercials American children see by age eigh-
teen: 350,000
The foregoing amount expressed in days (based on an average
of 40 seconds per commercial): 160.4

Number of TV sets . . .
    in 1947: 170,000
    in 1991: 750 million

CONNOISSEUR, SEPTEMBER 1989.

Percentage increase in income for over-65 households (senior citizens) between 1967 and 1987: 52.6
For all other households: 7

Percentage of males aged 30–34 married with spouse present . . .
    in 1960: 85.7
    in 1987: 64.7
Percentage of females aged 30–34 married with spouse present . . .
    in 1960: 88.7
    in 1987: 68.2

U.S. BUREAU OF THE CENSUS, CURRENT POPULATION REPORTS,
NO. 423, P. 20.

Percentage of U.S. 18–29 year olds who agree that "there is no point in staying at a job unless you are completely satisfied.": 58
Who disagree: 40

Percentage of U.S. 18–29 year olds who agree that "given the way things are, it will be much harder for people in my generation to live as comfortably as previous generations.": 65
Who disagree: 33

Percentage of U.S. 18–29 year olds who answered "yes" to the question "Would you like to have a marriage like the one your parents had?": 44
Who said "no": 55

FROM A TELEPHONE POLL OF 602 18-29-YEAR-OLD AMERICANS
TAKEN FOR TIME/CNN ON JUNE 13–17, 1990, BY YANKELOVICH
CLANCY SHULMAN, SAMPLING ERROR ±4%. AS REPORTED IN
TIME, JULY 16, 1990.